A high stakes game plays out magnificently against the deadly backdrop of the mystical Shirakami-Sanchi forest of Japan. In Katherine Nader's brilliant re-imagining of the Hunger Games, replete with highly original character-izations and complex plot twists make this sci fi thriller a must read."

Brent Fidler

"Dive into Japan's most historically-rich forest, where de-scendants of a royal samurai clan, the Ainu commune, a South Korean soldier, an American agent, and Japanese assassins work together to win The Foragers Contest."

GW

"Nader holds no punches in this thrilling tale set in the merciless forests of Japan. Witness battle royale with a twist as she expertly weaves flawed-yet-likeable charac-ters in a game where everybody's fighting for something, and nobody's letting up."

Brandon Young, Creator of *Planet Bastard*

The Foragers

The Foragers

THE SHIRAKAMI-SANCHI FOREST

Katherine Nader

Life Rattle Press

Published in Canada

Life Rattle Press
196 Crawford Street
Toronto, Ontario M6J 2V6

www.liferattle.ca

Life Rattle Press New Publishers Series
ISSN 1713 8981
ISBN: 978-1-987936-01-8

Cover design and Illustrations by Muzzammil Baig

Book design by Katherine Nader
www.katherinenader.com

"…I have given you the keys to the treasure, which others haven't got. But you must want to open the door. Do you want to go empty handed?"
–H.H. Shri Mataji Nirmala Devi

Contents

PREFACE 3

Chapter One 16

Chapter Two 37

Chapter Three 56

Chapter Four 77

Chapter Five 99

Chapter Six 117

Chapter Seven 133

Chapter Eight 146

Chapter Nine 160

Chapter Ten 177

Chapter Eleven 190

Chapter Twelve   **207**

Chapter Thirteen   **214**

Chapter Fourteen   **222**

Chapter Fifteen   **230**

Chapter Sixteen   **233**

EPILOGUE   **239**

"…I have given you the keys to the treasure, which others haven't got. But you must want to open the door. Do you want to go empty handed?"
–*H.H. Shri Mataji Nirmala Devi*

PREFACE

Someday, in the future,
I'll find myself running from the light
that shines in your empty heart,
and sets your soul ablaze.
The fireflies have flown off into the summer sky
never to return. Hotaru no haka,
The grave of the fireflies.

Hotaru no Haka, 1988

RAIN PELTS DOWN ON WOODEN DEBRIS and fallen timber, replenishing the soil of carbon-rich life forms on the forest floor. The wind filters through the trees, and the damp leaves rustle among the branches. The echoes and moans of the night storm howl among the hollowed trunks. Dogs bark in the distance. The sound of footsteps gets closer and closer. A hand rests on a moss-covered tree, its branches twisting down a slope near a black water lake. A blue light from a flip phone brightens a girl's face. Her black hair tangles from a braid. Sweat and rain drench her face and her moon-circled eyes cry with paranoia. Her wet fingers fiddle for numbers on the keypad. The dial tone goes out of service.

The girl dials again.

STATIC.

She cups her mouth to silence her whimpers, dials again and her fingers slip. The phone drops. The light goes out.

She screams.

Dogs bark and jump on the shadow against the tree.

SPLASH.

The girl floats into the water and sinks into the darkness of the lake.

***

"Shut it off." The Director, a man with two black hairs on his bald head, points to a young man sitting in front of a number of surveillance monitors. The young man pauses one screen, and the video stops right when the dogs began to bark at the water. The girl's body is nowhere to be seen. The Director takes a look at his watch and sighs.

"Let them in," he says into his com.

By the gate of a forest's base, a Kuma Hunter, dressed in black and strapped with receivers, leans into his earpiece. "Yes, Director."

He gestures to the rest of the Kuma Hunters, armed with hunting gear, and they help him open the gate. Hundreds of people wait on the other side.

"One by one, now," the Kuma Hunter says, guiding people in. Some shove each other, some bid their families and friends goodbye and others rush in while the Kuma Hunter counts them. All security cameras are on them and piano music starts to play from the mounted speakers.

"Welcome to the Shirakami-Sanchi forest," a feminine voice says, "known as Japan's White-God Mountain. The forest is over nine thousand years old, one of the first in the world to inhabit more than five hundred new and endangered species of flora and fauna..."

People line up in front of a dome structure with a 'security office' sign on it. Many others join them.

"Today marks the tenth anniversary of The Foragers Contest," the audio continues in the background. "For a chance to win one million dollars, you will need your ID to check-in at the front desk and collect your registration badge and kit."

Staff members in uniform scan IDs and register people in as contestants. "Here's a brochure and an instruction sheet," one says to a contestant as she hands him a kit.

He opens it to find one AA battery, a flare, a torch, and a screw.

"What did you get?" a friend in line asks.

"Nothing I need." He laughs.

"The contest runs annually for a period of one year," the feminine voice transmits through the speakers. A girl with short brown hair appears on multiple TV screens behind the front desk. "As a winner of TFC, I'm honored to welcome you home, where you will become successful at anything you do, where you will be whoever you need to be, and become the world's Ultimate Forager." The girl smiles on screen and it draws round after round of applause.

"That's Sharon," a contestant whispers to her friend. "I heard she joined at fifteen." She points to a sign. "See? It's fifteen plus only."

Other signs, labeled, 'Impermissible Items' show crossed out guns and chemicals.

"Hundred," the Kuma Hunter counts the last one in. He gestures for the other hunters to close the gate. The rest of the crowd rises in uproar, fighting for a way in. A man tries to climb over the fence.

"If you try to break in," the Kuma Hunter explains, resting an arm on his hunting rifle as a security camera turns towards the man, "you will be arrested for trespassing."

The man hauls himself over the fence and a number of Kuma Hunters tackle him down. They cuff his wrists behind his back.

"You just lost your chance of ever making it out of here alive," the Kuma Hunter whispers into the man's ear. He turns to the crowd behind the fence. "Let this be a lesson to you all. No one and I mean no one at any time is permitted to even so much as lay a finger on the premises. Is that clear?"

They drag the arrested man into the security office.

"Better luck next time." The Kuma Hunter winks at the crowd.

"How are we doing, Director?" Mrs. Kimura,

with short brown hair curled around her ears, enters from the only door of the surveillance room, blocking the sunlight behind her. Her ermine skin scarf dangles from her arms, its head resting in her palm. The Director gulps at the sight of the animal's bloody eye sockets.

"It's a new collection." She smiles. "Take a closer look." She raises her hand to the Director and turns the face of the animal to the side. "When a mamushi wraps itself around an animal, it reaches for its throat and squeezes tightly until…"

A drop of sweat trickles down the Director's bald head as he watches the woman squeeze the animal's head in her palm.

"POP!"

The Director jumps back, taking out a handkerchief to wipe his sweaty forehead. His hand quivers as he fails to recollect himself.

"Oh, come on, Director, it's not like it's the first time you've seen what we do—"

A man with a black hat walks in through the small door. A thin white line of light brightens the room and dims when he closes the door behind him.

"Ah, Hideki-san, you just missed out on a lovely story I was tel—"

"Where are we on the contestants?" Hideki-san walks past the woman with her ermine skin and bends over the young man to take a look at the changing screens in front of him. The young man pushes keys on the headboard, switching from one camera angle to the next until he lands on one angled down towards the line of contestants. A long-haired Kuma Hunter examines a contestant's fishing rod. The contestant, a teenage boy, looks off to the side as though he knows the camera is focused on him. He takes out a picture instead and shows it to the hunter. The hunter shrugs and returns the rod to the boy.

"Only twelve contestants left to check in, Sir," the young man answers.

"H-Hideki-san." The Director places a hand on his shoulder. Mr. Hideki, with a look of disapproval, straightens his back and brushes him off.

"My daughter?" he asks.

"Y-your … oh, yes! Your daughter." The Director folds the handkerchief and places it in his left pocket. "Your daughter was one of the first to check in.

Aya Hideki is doing just fine."

"Where's Mrs. Mori?"

"Aha, what I would do to see that woman's face." Mrs. Kimura crosses her arms.

"You behave yourself, Kimura-san," Hideki warns. "None of this would have happened if you had sought my advice."

"It's not the Kan's fault the fire in Italy got out of control."

"We lost many of our men, and if we had been more careful we wouldn't have to recruit so many contestants this year."

"That is if they survive." Mrs. Kimura giggles.

A tapping sound outside the room echoes over the steps that lead to the door. The knob shakes into place and turns. A woman bandaged around the eyes walks into the room, a walking cane tapping in front of her feet. She closes the door behind her.

"Oh no, Mrs. Mori, what in the world could have happened to you? How could you have survived such a terrible accident?" Mrs. Kimura covers a smile on her face.

"We both know that the fire was no accident,"

she says. "Not even your own husband's death makes up for the loss of our allies. We lost a major shareholder that night, Kimura-san. The Italian family that we have known for hundreds of years no longer exists, all because of one tiny mistake."

"You mean the plan where we add a little fire and give the Italians a scare, so that they can come back running to you for help?" Mrs. Kimura rubs her fingers against her thumb, hinting at money.

Mrs. Mori unsheathes a dagger from her cane and slices the animal's head from the ermine skin in Mrs. Kimura's palm. "Don't mock me, Kimura-san." She wipes the blood off the blade with her finger. She sniffs it, scrubs it off with her thumb and says, "Hmm, so fresh. A recent kill, I believe. Next time, it'll be your head—"

"Oi, oi," the Director interrupts. He rests a hand on the blind woman's arm. "Mori-san, Kimura-san, the Italian family got what they deserve, so let's not talk about the past and focus on the contest that is about to start." The Director claps his hands. "While we let the contestants think there's a money prize for the winners, Hideki-san promised you get to choose whichever contestants to recruit for your clan. Isn't that exciting?"

The Director exchanges glances between the two. No one moves. Hideki-san finally slips his hand around Mrs. Kimura's arm and backs her away. Mrs. Kimura relaxes her shoulders, snickers, and hangs onto him.

"Sometimes I wonder whose side you're on, Hideki-san." Mrs. Mori withdraws the blade and sheaths it into her cane.

Hideki-san's lips stretch to the side, but he doesn't smile.

"Nikki-chan!" the Director yells.

"Hai!" A head bangs against the table of monitors. Nikki crawls from underneath and rubs her head. The young man at the screen wheels out of her way. Nikki finishes plugging two cables together. "All done." She rises, carrying a black red-headed woodpecker in her hand, upright and unmoving. She stares at everyone in front of the Director. "Oh, I made this one. It's my new invention … and yes, I will go announce that we're starting." She smiles.

Nikki leaves the room, stepping out of the RV and into the security office's back parking lot. She sits on the steps of the RV, placing the bird on its feet, and pushes her finger in between the tail feathers to pull a string. The bird's eyelids flip open. A camera lens inside the bird's pupil zooms in and out. Once focused, the bird preps its wings, flies and lands on the roof of the security office.

Nikki gives it a thumbs-up. Her other hand cups the side of her face.

The Director sees Nikki on one of the screens.

"All good." Nikki hears him in her earpiece.

She heads to the platform in the center of the field in front of the security office. She nods to the Kuma Hunters, lining up with their backs against the fence, and picks up the megaphone off the ground. One hundred contestants look up from their scattered spots. Kits and instructions lay in their hands. Nikki examines the face of each and every contestant, as she spins around in a circle. She eyes Aya Hideki, who hides her nose in a white scarf and stands behind one of her personal bodyguards. Many new faces, among previous contestants', ponder at Nikki, one of them being a middle-aged American. Nikki marvels if he understands Japanese. The digital clock displays sixty hours at the roof of the security office.

"Contestants!" Nikki announces as some of the contestants cheer. "You've made it to the initial round. Congratulations. To successfully complete this round, you're going to need one registration badge: yours, your predator's and/or your prey's. You may use your kits at any time to assist you. Any further questions can be answered here." Nikki raises a sample instructions sheet. "You can either work together or alone for a chance to win one million dollars. You have sixty hours to complete the initial round," Nikki cheers into the megaphone, as the contestants steady their foothold.

"Good luck everyone!"

The countdown starts and the contestants scatter. Some sprint into the forest and others chase after each other as they all clear out of the base. Only one steers clear from the field: a young boy with a fishing rod leaning over the branch of a beech tree. He brings his binoculars up to see a blind woman leaving the RV. Two others follow her out and they each get into their personal cars. The boy puts down his binoculars and stares at a picture of a man. He flips it over to reveal three others: two women and a man smiling and working together in a lab. The boy feels Nikki's eyes on him. He exchanges one look with her and disappears.

CHAPTER ONE

Fisher

RAIN PELTED DOWN ON WOODEN DEBRIS, re-plenishing the soil of carbon-rich life forms on the forest floor. The wind filtered through the trees, the damp leaves rustled among the branches, and the echoes and moans rumbling inside hollowed trunks came to a stop. I poked my head out of a tree, admiring the view of the forest below me. I spotted a pagoda miles away, its red roof pointing through the canopy, and turning around I saw a white snag tree struck by lightning years ago—or so the legends said. As the weight of the rain lifted, clouds cleared from the peaks of the mountains.

If only Mom could see this.

I tightened the strap of my fishing rod around

my bag and slid down the branches. The snap of a twig cranked my head around and I felt a prick against my neck. All sensation left my body and I plummeted into the leaves, landing onto the highest, spongiest, and shortest branch.

SNAP!

Everything turned to black.

***

I slashed the rice plants with my sickle, my boots sinking ankle-deep into the water. The sun scorched my back as I arched down to gather the grains into my basket. The mid-summer weather had been rough on us this year. We barely had enough food on the table, and mother had stopped eating to make sure there was enough for me.

"Shouta!" A voice jerked my head around. I saw a woman with a straw hat and a basket in arm, waving her hand at me.

"Tanaka-san?" I brought a hand to my forehead and shielded my eyes from the sun.

"Isoide! It's your mother!"

The sickle slipped from my hands, and I tossed

the basket to the ground. I ran across the rice field, through a yard and into a wooden hut. "Mother!" I yelled, taking off my boots and sliding the door open. I heard her cough inside. I hopped into the kitchen, grabbing a jar of water off the counter and hurried into Mom's room. She lay frail in bed, her blue veins visible under her skin. A profound sadness grew every time I saw her, fatigue engraved on her worn face. I could no longer see that desire, that fire in her eyes. All that remained was a hollowness reflected in her, with no room for her true self anymore. "Don't get up," I told her as she shuffled under her covers. Blood stained the tissues in her hand. That was always the scariest thing, knowing that the virus could take her from me any minute.

"You're not ready yet, my son," she said in a weak voice.

"Not ready for what? For what?"

I woke up.

I squinted from the blinding sun, my eyelids heavy and my mouth dry and sticky with thick saliva. A branch hung crookedly from the tree above.

What happened?

I brushed away the wet leaves that grimed my

skin, and raising my head up. Brown weasels that had been licking at my red hand scurried into the hole of a fallen tree. I gazed at my hand, not feeling any pain or finding any cuts.

Was this my blood?

I rubbed my sore neck to find an empty dart, a yellow drop of goo oozing out of it. I glanced at my watch, cracked in its center, and panicked. I was out for a whole day? I struggled to free myself from the yew bushes that caught me, my green army trousers still tangled and stained from the squished red yew berries. I instinctively reached for my left breast pocket and a pang of horror hit me.

My badge!

My eyes landed on a journal, clothes, fishing rod and a kit having been dumped out of my bag and onto the wood chips. "No," I croaked, losing my balance and tumbling to my knees. The ground whirled around me. It felt like an inflated balloon mounted pressure under my cranium. I closed my eyes and braced myself for what was to come next. My body shook as though it plunged once more through the air, two meters above the ground. Birds fluttered away when I cried.

It was a memory…or as I liked to call it, a vibe of a memory. I felt for my things on the ground but no memories came with it. I couldn't vibe into anything. The more I tried, squeezing my things hard, and forcing my attention on it, the more my stomach lurched. Chunks of food in a creamy chyme finally propelled into the air and splattered onto the ground. I heaved again and once more sprayed the ground with bubbling bile. My stomach contracted and I grabbed my burning throat. I coughed and leaned forward and let the last of it dribble from my lips. Sweat engulfed me, and trembling all over I collapsed against the tree for support. The dart lay in the wooden chips, its fletching made of feathers, and its inner casing lined with goo. I fumbled for it and brought it close to my face. I looked at my watch again. Two days left. I had two days left to make it out of here alive. I took a deep breath and held it in.

Faint rays of sun peeked through the entanglement of branches and beech trees around me. The light and shadows danced on my skin. I closed my eyes to think. The pecking of the spotted nutcracker with a mix of squirrel calls filled the air. A cool breeze ran behind my ears and through my hair.

Think.

My watch ticked. I held my breath as the next wave of heat washed over me.

"There's nothing here," a voice said. Three white semi-blurred faces with freckled skin and blonde hair, stared down at me. They blended into one when they spoke.

"They must have gotten his badge first," one said, polishing his blow gun and carrying darts in one hand. An upturned smile formed on his face as he laughed.

"Shall we kill him?" another said, joining in.

"He's already dead," the third added.

A surge of air snapped me out of my inner state.

"No," I groaned. If they didn't take my badge, who did? A flinching headache spread across my temple. I reached for my right pocket and tugged on a small yellow note. With this, I wouldn't have to go home. With this, I could make it to the next round of the competition. With this, I could find Dad. I grinned and picked up my journal from the ground. I opened it to make sure Dad's picture was still inside the flap. I couldn't believe how none of the Kuma Hunters recognized him after so many years since he disappeared. I tossed everything back inside the bag and strapped my fishing pole to it. I tracked down the weasels' prints in the mud, and followed them to a stream called The Anmon River. The big brown weasel and its cubs stood on a rock at one end of the current. They each waved a paw at the water. I set my things down and looked at my reflection. Dried mud stuck to the ends of my short black hair. I looked just as young as my dad was in the picture. I imagined greying hair on my head and a scar under my left eye, slanted down like an arrow pointing to my lips. I focused on my dad and his scar, feeling it burn into my head. With the pain came memories. And a voice: "Our village is under attack."

I could see it again. The Kuma Hunter carrying a man with a bleeding face into my home. Mother falling to her knees in tears. My hands trembling from the fear.

"Was it the bears again?" I'd asked.

"You shouldn't be here," the Kuma Hunter warned.

"Go back to your room, my son," Mother urged,

sliding the paper-walled doors shut. I pressed my ears to the walls and listened.

"Aomori is filled with bears," the Kuma Hunter said. "You shouldn't live here with a child of his age."

"We have nowhere else to go! He may be eight but he's strong like his father," Mother said. "Come on, Haruki...stay with us."

I squeezed my eyes shut, letting the memory abate. It was no good to dwell on the past. Staring back into my reflection, I wondered if I would recognize my dad when I saw him.

What did his scar look like now?

Taking a deep breath, I stepped into the water and marched onto the rocks that extended across the river. A stream of yellow ayu, red char fish, and black and white spotted iwana trout swam together. My stomach growled as I watched the red char fish jump over the small rocks against the stream and dive back down. I looked to the end of the trail of rocks where the big weasel lay. A red char fish jumped and the weasel caught it. I watched the stream on my end and laid my hands above the rocks. The fish wriggled past my legs, as though my existence held no threat to them. They were fearless in the absence of predators. If fish went missing one by one, their population wouldn't notice. By the time a fish identified its predator, it would be too late to warn the others because then it would be eaten, just as my badge number was taken. I was just like the fish here, not knowing who my predator was.

A red char fish finally jumped into my hand. I squeezed my fingers around it and watched it wriggle between my palms. I looked for the big weasel to show me what to do next, but it walked back to the other side with the dead fish in its mouth. I stared right into the eye of the fish, wondering if it could see me. Its eyes bulged out from the pressure. I took a deep breath, guilt ingraining itself into my mind. I closed my eyes to think. I felt the fish's hunger, merging with mine.

Vibing into things that didn't think was easy. Humans were more complicated. I pictured the taste of its white flesh on my tongue, and salivated at the thought of it. It was either the fish or me dying of starvation. I impulsively smacked its head against the rock so it wouldn't warn the others. Blood oozing out of its neck made me regret it after.

"Someone's going to catch us!" a feminine voice echoed in the woods.

I dropped the fish into my bag, and sank into the water, my head hidden just behind the rocks. A woman and a man emerged from the bushes. The woman pointed at the fire and gestured with her other hand at the man to put it out. The man's wet black hair plastered to his face as he bent down and dropped a few sticks into a pile. He rolled up his sleeves and opened his kit.

"What are you doing?" the woman yelled at him.

"Gum?" he asked. She shook her head and he popped it into his mouth. I watched him chew and my stomach knotted. The man then grabbed a stick and rubbed it against the bark of a tree. He brought it closer to his face and smiled. "That should do it." He tossed it back into the pile of wood. He took the gum wrapper and put it on both ends of a battery. A fire ignited in the middle and spread across the sticks.

"Pine sap," the man laughed.

"Is this your plan?" The woman crossed her arms.

"Stop worrying, Koko." The man stuck his hands out to dry. "I'm sure we lost them. Besides, even if they found us, what's the worst that can happen? They're just going to ask for our badges and all we have to do is say no."

"We're in the middle of a forest." The woman stomped towards the river. "They could do anything to us and no one will ever know."

"Honey, they would be smart not to leave dead bodies in a forest, otherwise this whole place would be shut down," the man said. "Come on, if contestants had actually been killing each other all this time, you think we wouldn't know about it? This is the real world we're talking about here."

Koko filled up her blue hat with water. She spun around and held her hat over the fire.

"What are you doing?" The man jolted from his spot and grabbed her wrists.

"Move," Koko said. A shadow moved through the forest. The hat slipped from the woman's grasp and she grabbed her bag.

"You thought you could run away forever?" A rough voice came from the rustling bushes.

The man sprawled onto the ground, digging his heels into the mud. He burned his elbow on the fire and grasped his arm in pain. Koko screamed for him to run as she disappeared into the forest.

More shadows turned up.

"Go after her," the man from the bushes ordered. The men that stood behind him nodded. I counted three of them, as they went after the woman.

"Take it easy, Shima, matte gureyo..." The man on the ground cowered by the fire. "It-it's just a game."

Shima walked out of the shade, his face shadowed by a baseball cap. He dressed like a hitchhiker and carried a black backpack equipped with mountain-climbing ropes.

"Is that your wife who abandoned you?" Shima asked.

"She's not my wife," the man replied. One of Shima's friends, with long brown hair and glasses, grabbed the man when he tried to escape.

My fists tightened and I wanted to help, but my body wouldn't move. Jamming my knee into the sand, my shoulders shook in the water. Mother was right, I wasn't ready to join her.

With a sharp kunai pointed at the man's throat, Shima's friend pulled out a badge from the man's jacket pocket. "Twenty-one," he said.

"That would make your wife twenty-two," Shima

smirked and rested his hand on his friend's shoulder. "Jun, bring him with us. His wife will come back for him."

They picked up the couple's bags. Jun dragged the weak man, and they disappeared through the bushes. I waited a few moments and exhaled, realizing I had been barely breathing. I didn't even want to vibe into seeing what these men would do to me if they found me. Taking comfort in the burning fire, I backed away from the rocks, swam toward its warmth, took the red char fish out of my pocket, and skewered it over the flames.

"Itadakimasu," I breathed, thanking God for humbly receiving this food, then nibbled on the fish. From the stirring bushes, a man's blue eyes stared deeply into mine. He was covered in dirt, as if he'd just climbed out of a hole. Fear crippled me, and my legs couldn't run. Entirely soaked, I held out my only means of defense—the skewer.

"I don't have my badge," I said. The man's presence towered over me. His eyes shone, his shoulders relaxed, and he laughed. Shame sank in and my face reddened with anger. I read sixty-four on his dirty badge. It hung from his chest like he was challenging his predator for a fight rather than hid-ing.

"I'm not after you, boy," he said, stepping towards me. I backed away. The man sighed. He walked past me and bent down to the river. "What's your name?"

I didn't answer. The skewer in my hand almost snapped. Get him, a voice kept telling me. What is wrong with you?

The man washed his face and I gradually recognized him as an American.

"I'm Nick." He turned around and offered his hand. When I hesitated, he sighed and added, "Do you speak English? Did you see a group of men pass by here with badge numbers like…this one?" Nick reached for his belt pocket. I picked up a rock from the ground.

"Easy." Nick gestured for me to lower my weap-on. "It's just paper." Nick unfolded a yellow piece of paper with nine on it. Hooks and wires hung from his waist.

"AHH!"

Both of our heads jerked towards the sound. The scream scared off some birds in the distance.

"I guess they found his wife," Nick said and put

the paper back in his pocket. "Good luck to you, kid."

I fixed my eyes on him until he disappeared into the woods. My chest felt heavy. I dropped to my knees and punched the wet soil.

I let him walk away from me!

My body shook as the effect of the drug in the dart took its toll on me again. I collapsed by the fire. A crumpled yellow note fell out of my hand. I stared at its center and slipped into darkness again.

By the time I opened my eyes, orange rays filled the purple-blue sky. I turned over onto my side to find a bright red bird with a yellow belly nibbling on a fish bone a few inches away. My eyes widened in disbelief. Every muscle in me froze as I admired the rare animal. I rummaged through my bag quietly and pulled out the journal, flipping through the pages. My finger landed on a drawing of a king-fisher. I had never seen one this big and up close before. Its red beak and yellow throat marked it as a male. He sniffed the ground till his bill uncovered another fishbone from the soil. The fisher clasped the fishbone with his bill and his head snapped in the direction of the water. He flew up fast. If it weren't for his bright red color, I would've lost sight of him. He rose ten meters above the water's surface and kept his head perfectly still. The fluttering of his wings quickened, allowing him to stay in one place without actually moving. His tail beat in the air and kept his body stationary. The wings flapped several times per second. The bird's head froze. His bill remained shut as he waited in silence.

SPLASH.

The bird plunged into the water and rose up with a big red fish in his bill. He flew above my head—close enough for me to see a smaller fish in the big fish's mouth. It rendered me speechless, unable to comprehend what had just occurred. I glanced into the water to find a number of big red char fish devouring smaller ones.

It's infanticide, a voice in my head said. I turned to see a man with a scar slanted up when he smiled.

I felt like I was eight again.

"Dad, is that you?" I said. Please let it be real, please let it be real.

"I'll take this," the man said. He took a small red char fish from my little hands and tied it to the hook of his fishing line. "They make great bait. Big fish love to prey on the young, just as the rich and powerful feed off the rest of us. These fish are going to wipe out their entire population one day." He lowered his line into the water. "The trick is to identify the prey and predator. Only then you can win."

The fishing line tightened.

"The best way of attack is to make sure the prey is unaware of being hunted."

I stared at the smoke rising from the burnt out fire. When I turned, the man was gone and the vibe left with him. I wiped my wet eyes. All my worries lost their sting, and hope filled my heart again. Perhaps it had been there all along, trapped by my sorrow.

"Thank you, dad," I said. Returning to my bag, I pulled my fishing rod out of its case. I tested the line, adjusted the hook into place, and an idea formed in my head. I refused to be powerless. I took my steps carefully by the mud tracks. The path had become slick under the rain, the only clues to the ruts being the puddles. It rose steeply ahead. Narrow rocky passes covered the path, with the mud prints no more than a mild disturbance in the soil. Amidst the bushes, a thin wire stretched over the ground. I bent down to examine it and saw Koko's emptied bags tossed into a bush. With one touch, I could see what had happened. I walked over the trap until there were no more prints, just another wire stretched an inch above the ground. I heard footsteps approaching and found my way up the nearest hornbeam. One of the hitchhiker's men stood below me. He crouched down and examined my prints.

"Jun," a voice called. Jun turned around and triggered the wire. It made a clicking sound. The man looked down at his foot and the rope tightened like a noose around his ankle. It yanked him from the leg to the lower tree branch of the hornbeam I was camouflaged in.

"Hey! What is going on?!" Jun barked. "Get me out of this thing!"

A black backpack landed in the middle of the open ground, empty of its mountain climbing ropes. I looked in the direction it came from. A tall man with big blue eyes stepped through the bushes, a belt of muddied tools dropped from his waist. He rolled up his sleeves and I saw his badge. Nick. He reached into the pocket of the man tied upside down and pulled out a badge.

"What?!" Nick gasped. I peered through the hornbeam leaves to get a better look at the number and almost fell. Air lodged into my throat and a tremor came over me. In the eye of my mind, I saw a security office.

"Have you seen this man?" I showed a picture to a long-haired Kuma Hunter.

The Kuma Hunter took the picture, shrugged, and pressed it against my chest, right where my badge was tucked in.

"You'd better get going," he said. "You don't want to be late."

I snapped out of it, realizing that the Kuma Hunter was Jun. He took my badge before the contest even started! I watched Nick hold badge eighty-eight in his hand.

"Where's badge number nine?" Nick lowered his head down to the man's face, a few inches above the ground. "I saw you holding it! Where did you put it?"

Nick's prey laughed hysterically. "You think I'm crazy enough to carry bait on me?"

Nick desperately searched the other bags.

"Where did you get this?" He held up badge eighty-eight only for it to be snatched away by a hook.

"What the..."

I reeled in the thick fishing line and aimed for Nick's badge this time. The hook latched onto the pin. Nick looked down at his chest. I pulled on the fishing line over the tree branch and jumped to the ground. The pin tore through Nick's shirt, and the badge flew up into the tree, over the branch, and landed in my hand. I now had two badge numbers: sixty-four and eighty-eight.

"You…" Nick choked on his words.

I pulled out my yellow piece of paper. Nick noticed the number.

"Sixty-four?" He took a step towards me as if the truth finally hit him. "Wait!" Nick called when I climbed onto a branch. "You didn't tell me your name."

I looked deep into the Shirakami-Sanchi forest, feeling lighter than before. Just as the bird caught the predatory fish distracted by its own prey, I did the same. The forest's red creatures welcomed me.

"Fisher," I said. "It's Fisher."

CHAPTER TWO

Celio

"SHH …" I PLACED ONE FINGER OVER MY LIPS AND pointed to the horned white and grey animal near the white snag tree. Eli poked her little golden head through the bushes. We both watched the serow munch on light brown mushrooms.

"It's beautiful!" Eli gasped. "Celio, look!"

The serow's ears stiffened. Its furry head froze. Eli covered her mouth with her child-like hands. We listened to the sound of our breathing. The serow's mouth twitched. Its red tongue licked its grey snout.

Eli plucked blue flowers from the bushes, stacked the petals on top of each other and squeezed them. "Do you think she eats flowers?"

I brushed an arrow past Eli's chestnut hair. She heard it click into place through the cut notch in a paintbrush.

"It's amazing what you can do with a spoon and a rock," I said, looking over my empty kit. It didn't take me long to file the spoon they had given me into a sharp metal broadhead. All I needed was a slingshot and paintbrush to make the bow.

"You can't!" Eli covered the arrow with her hand.

"But we have to eat." I pinched the arrow nock in the slingshot pouch, pulled back, and aimed it again towards the serow.

"The Kuma Hunters said we can only hunt bears!" Eli stood up. The serow leaped past the white tree, over the bushes and into the green beech trees.

"No!" I jumped out from our hideout and sprinted after the animal. Bushes rustled, leaves fell and the serow vanished. I turned back to Eli. "See what you've done?"

"But we can only hunt b—"

"Who cares? We can just say a bear ate it, Dios mío, Eli." I packed the bow and three arrows into the kit. "How are we going to eat now? That serow could've lasted us till tomorrow night before the competition ends."

Eli crouched over the arched roots of a dead white tree and tugged on mushrooms from its moist shade.

"Why don't we try those? They look like the Shii-take mushrooms mom used to make."

"Are you listening to me?" I slapped the mushrooms from Eli's hand. "They could be poisonous."

"But the serow was eating from—"

"I don't care what the serow was eating! I want meat." I stomped on the mushrooms.

Eli's face turned red. She looked down at the petals in her hand and tears quivered in her eyes.

"Winning is what will guarantee our survival," I said. "There's no life for us in Italy, not after the fire that killed our parents. Perdonami." I patted Eli's head. I released my foothold on the mushrooms and picked them up for her. "Forget the serow. We'll find something else to eat."

Eli's wrist brushed against her eyes and her sleeve pulled back to reveal thin streaks of burns. "Okay." Eli looked back at the white tree behind her. "Why is the tree white, Celio?"

"Because it's dead. Now come on, let's go." I

hauled the straps of the bag over my shoulder and hung a water pouch from my neck.

Eli approached the fallen white branches of the tree and scattered the blue flower petals across it. "It doesn't look dead anymore." Eli stepped backwards. Her eyes never left the life she created.

My ears picked up the sound of a stream. "Eli, give me the compass … The compass, Eli! If you paid more attention you wouldn't have lost the map I made." I snatched Eli's red bag, dug my hand through it, and felt the coolness of the metal. I pulled back the compass hanging from a chain. Its gold glinted in the light. I turned it to find an inscription on the back.

To the finest forager...

The needle pointed north. I picked up my pace, unscrewing the cap on my water pouch and running down the hill. Eli caught up behind me. A two meter high waterfall rumbled beside me. A sign towered on top of a rocky ridge.

Anmon no Taki (Shadow Gate Falls).

I dropped to my knees, plunged my face into the water and drank as much as I possibly could. I gasped as my head broke the surface. "Phew! Thank god we made it." I filled the water pouch and tossed it to Eli. She drank it as she sat on the rocks. I unzipped my light rain jacket and dropped it on the wooden chips and autumn leaves of the wet soil.

"What are you doing?" Eli tied the water pouch to her bag.

I kicked off my muddy boots. My belt clanked against the ground when I dropped my trousers. I tightened the red band of the kunai around my thigh, a few inches below my drawers. Eli stared at the spider symbol on my blade. It looked just like the one from the storybook.

"We fought the Kan for them," mother, with long chestnut hair read from it one night. It had a spider symbol on its cover.

"And what's this?" Eli, nine at the time, pulled back her blanket and pointed to a picture of a bald man with a katana in a wheel chair surrounded by parents and their children.

"The Mori Family." The woman smiled, tucking Eli back in bed. "They are descendants of the royal samurai clan, remember? The one who fought the assassins to protect Japan's seventy-seventh Emperor?"

Eli yawned.

"But, that's a story for another time." The woman closed the story book and kissed Eli's forehead. "Goodnight, my sweet child."

"Mom," I said, climbing into the bed across from Eli's. "What if the assassins were to come back?"

Mom's concern diminished with a smile. "The Mori owe us their lives. They will be there to protect us."

"But, what if—"

"Celio," Mom sighed. "It's your first day of Middle School tomorrow. Shouldn't you be in your own bed?"

"I know." I rolled my eyes. "But, there's like twenty other bedrooms! Can't I just sleep in this one? Eli would like that. Besides, if she has any more nightmares, I can be here for her."

"All right, Celio." Mom kissed my forehead. "Just this once." She kindled the fire in the fireplace and dimmed the lights in our room.

The burns on my back tingled as I remembered the fire burning Eli's bedroom. The storybook was gone, along with everything and everyone else we ever cared about. I ran up the rocks behind Eli, clapped my hands above my head and dove into the water.

"I want to swim!" Eli bent down to unlace her pink boots.

"It's too deep. You can't swim," I warned her as I swam farther away. "Besides, what will you do if people see you? It's not like you have another set of clothes."

Eli pouted. She brushed the leaves off my jacket, and clasped it tight against her chest. We had used the last of our money to forge Eli's ID and fly over here.

"I'll be back soon. I promise." I ducked my head under the water, swam towards the falls and climbed on top of a green algae rock. Fish nibbled at the algae, while others wiggled away. I ran my fingers through my long chestnut hair, opened my arms wide to the water shower, tip toed around in a circle and back flipped into the water. Kinko fish sucked at the dead skin on my feet. It tickled.

"Get away from me!" I splashed them away, kicking and swirling at the water until someone laughed.

"Who's there?" I stood up. The water levelled up

to my waist. I turned left and right of the falls. A pebble hissed through the air and splashed into the water in front of me. I looked up. A girl with a ponytail leaned her head over the rocks at the top of the falls. She stood over the ridge, staring down at me with green snake eyes. My back burned, my face turned red and I crossed my arms over my chest.

"It's very rude to spy on people. Who are you?" I lowered myself back into the water until it reached my neck.

"Elinka."

"What? How do you know that name?"

The girl's moon-shaped eyes reflected a red-or-ange flame. She pointed beyond the falls, the red marks of an hourglass on her wrist. I peered over to the right end of the river and saw my jacket hang-ing over the rock. "Eli?"

I looked back up at the ridge. It was deserted. I scrambled out of the water and towards the rock where my jacket lay. Eli's footprints were near my boots and pants, but our bags were gone. "Eli?!" My voice echoed in the forest. I unstrapped the kunai and dressed myself again. Heading down the side of the river, I stabbed the blade in between the shadow gate rocks, climbed the slope of the hill, grabbed onto roots and branches, and pulled myself up to the top. My vision suddenly spinning, I closed my eyes and continued up the stream.

I found no traces of the ponytailed girl—not even footprints. Everything remained still until a shadow stirred in the corner of my eye. I aimed my kunai at it. It cut through the air till it hit the trunk of a tree. Leaves fell at the impact. I approached the wriggling, camouflaged viper trapped by my blade, released my weapon from the bark and watched the true yellow and brown-striped colors of the snake return as it suffered a seizure from the wound behind its eyes. White fluid from the glands behind its eyes engulfed the blade. It steamed. The blade turned black.

A mamushi?! I gasped.

I shoved the dead snake away with my left hand and loosened the kunai from it. The transparent fluid dried up. Only rat snakes had brown stripes, but could the mamushi camouflage into this color too? Rat snakes in beech forests were non-venomous, but what if this one was?

I gnawed at the snake's rough neck and chewed slowly.

Yuck! I spat it out. This is not meat.

I wiped my drooling lips with the sleeve of my jacket and continued to march. A scream ushered me into the right direction.

"So, little girl," a woman's voice ricocheted from the wall of orange and grey rocks behind her. A white scarf dangled from her neck and over her black leather jacket. She wore heeled boots and had a camera with a plastic bag around the lens pointed at them. "Where are the badge numbers?"

A man pulled on Eli's hair and seized her hands behind her back. A cemented path spread under their feet where the bags were emptied.

The woman sighed. She turned off her camera.

"Speak!" The woman slapped Eli's cheek. Her long red nails carved bloody trails through Eli's skin.

"Don't touch her!" I threw my blade at the woman. It slashed her palm, clattered against the cold stone behind her and clanked onto the cold-footed ground.

The woman's head snapped towards me ten feet away. She sucked the blood from the side of her palm and licked her lips.

"Celio, I didn't tell them anythi—" Eli shrieked, as the man pulled on her hair tighter.

"Let my sister go."

"Ho ho, Juro." The woman smirked at the man. "The boy has the courage to tell me what to do … tfeh!" She spat. Her tanned features and semi-circled eyes revealed that she wasn't a local. "Nani o mite, boya?"

I cursed under my breath and dug my hand into my jacket pocket.

"Looks like you're running out of weapons!" The woman kicked my kunai into the stream.

"No!" My body quivered.

"It's … simple. You give me your badges and I … I I-let the girl go."

I crept towards the black-haired woman. She was just like me: scared. Sweat tickled down her forehead. She loosened the scarf and scratched her swelling neck.

"W-what's happening to … me …" The woman's eyes rolled to the back of her head, her legs wobbled and she fainted. I caught her and lowered her to the ground. The man had his arms around Eli, holding the bow I had made.

"Stay back." I picked up one of my arrows on the ground and held it tight against the woman's neck. "The blade was poisoned by a viper's venom," I explained. "I don't know how much time your, uh, friend has."

The shocked man staggered. His cheeks whitened. "Ojosama hanashite gure!" The man gestured with his hands repeatedly to explain his language.

"My sister," I stated. "Release." I gestured back.

"Ojosama." The man pointed to the girl in my arms. "Tasukete." He pushed Eli towards me.

"Eli, it's okay, just pick up the bag and come here." I watched Eli's tears trickle down her face and onto her hands. The strap of a bag slipped twice from her trembling hands. The man continued to point the bow at me. I gestured for both of us to drop our weapons at the same time. "At the count of three, Eli …"

Eli nodded.

"Itchi … ni …" the man counted when I rose two of my fingers. "San."

"Run!" I backed away from the woman. The man dropped my bow and rushed to her side. I latched the arrow into the bow on the ground and aimed it at the man's back.

"Stop!" Eli threw herself in front of my poised bow. She stretched her arms out to block my aim. "He's more worried about the girl than his own life."

I peered over Eli's shoulder and at the two people on the ground. The girl shivered with cold sweats. Her pupils rolled to the back of her head and the red veins in her white sockets bulged. "I don't care." I shoved past Eli. "They could've killed you."

"But they didn't!" Eli's tears rolled down her cheeks.

"Ojosama tasukete!" the man begged.

"I … I can't help you." I shook my head. "I don't even know what poison or what snake did that. Let's go, Eli, before he calls attention to more of his men." I grabbed Eli's wrist.

"No!" She snatched her arm away. "There's no one else; it's just them."

A cold hand pulled on my trousers. "Puh-pulee-zu." The man was crawling on his knees, his hands clasped together in prayer.

"That's the first English word you've said." I lowered my bow. "We need to make a fire."

***

Cold water squeezed out of a white sheet over the sickly Ojosama. Eli felt the girl's forehead with her hand. The man tightened his grasp around Ojosama's hand and stared into the evening sky every few moments to pray.

"What is he saying?" Eli toasted the skewered mushrooms over the fire. "He keeps calling her Ojosama. That doesn't sound like a name. Maybe he's her bodyguard? Do you think he likes her?"

"He looks old enough to be her dad." I took the girl's camera apart and angled the camera lens towards a pile of wood. After a few moments, the light piercing through it ignited a fire. I lowered an arrow into the flames.

"Okay, move." I pushed Eli aside and carried the arrow over to Ojosama's swollen hand where the blue gash spread open. The dried blood crisped on the edges of the skin. "Hold her still," I told the man, and applied weight over Ojosama's arms. I pressed the side of the arrow into the gash.

Ojosama's eyes flew open and she screamed.

Smoke rose from her wound. The flesh melted together and the dried blood oozed from the heat.

"She swallowed some of the poison too." I loosened the scarf around the girl's neck. "That's strange."

"What?" Eli asked.

"The rash, it's gone."

I eyed the man watching over the girl and cupped my mouth. "When I was looking for you," I whispered to Eli, "I saw a mamushi..."

Eli gasped. "Like the one from the storybook?"

"Yes, the Kan did a lot of research on them. Either Ojosama is immune, or I killed a rat snake that looked like a mamushi."

I wrapped the scarf tightly around Ojosama's hand. Her face dampened with tears and sweat. I stood up and walked over to the river.

"Celio doesn't like to see people cry," Eli explained.

"You can let go of her hand now," I called to the man. "Come over here and help me find my kunai."

I untied my boots and rolled up my pants. The water reached my knees at the slope before the waterfall. The low current had slowed down after sunset and settled below the wall of rocks that barricaded the waterfall. I left my rain jacket with Eli, kept my white collared shirt on and hoped to find the blade before the last rays of sun died out. The man jumped into the water and swam downstream.

"Oi!" The man waved for me to come.

I squinted through the water to see what he was pointing at. Red fish swam up, their tails wagging behind them. A red band floated through the rocks at the bottom. I clasped my fingers around the band and pulled. A ball of slime came loose in my hand. It was a red slippery fish. I turned to the fire and drooled.

"Oww …" I pulled my leg away from another red fish that pinched me, bent down into the water and the fish wriggled out of my clasp. It followed a smaller red fish near my leg and swam away. I wondered if they were related, like Eli and I.

I laughed.

The man scooted over to me and peered into the water.

"I think these fish hate me." I reached for the red band again and pulled. "It's not coming out. The blade is trapped."

The man gestured for me to move. He lowered his hand deep into the water, straightened back up, raised a finger, as though to give him a minute, and swam to the fire. He searched through his kit behind the rocks, brought back a screw and a rock with him and motioned for me to take care of Ojosama. When I arrived at the fire, I turned back. The man hammered at the rocks.

Eli slept with her head over her bag. She lay flat on her back near Ojosama and held a bitten mushroom in her hand. I nibbled at it and froze. I grabbed some more from the skewer and felt nourished.

"I guess mushrooms do taste beefy. It'll do." I patted Eli's head. The fire reminded me of home.

"Run!" a ponytailed girl had yelled as the flames burned down our library.

A pillar had broken loose from the roof and the girl shoved me and Eli out of the way. "Get out of here!" She screamed as the fire engulfed her.

"W-what about you?" I yelled back. "Our parents?"

"I'm sorry..." A tear rolled down the side of her face. A man with long black hair wrapped his arm around her neck as they both disappeared into the fire.

A shiver ran down my back. I wondered if the girl from the fire and the girl from the waterfall were one and the same. I dried myself up, put on my jacket and took Eli's bag. If the Mori Clan really did abandon us in that fire, at least there was one person who had fought for us. I snuck behind the rocks to search the man and Ojosama's bags, keeping an eye on the man hammering away at the rocks. I found badge seven next to a yellow note, like the one we had, and flipped it over. It had the number fifteen in its center: Eli's badge. I rummaged through the man's bag even further and found no other badges. I slipped everything else in the false bottom of Eli's bag and returned to the fir, slinging our bags over Eli's shoulder.

A hand wrapped around my ankle.

I turned to Ojosama on the ground.

"Thank you," she said.

I freed my leg. "I didn't do it for you." I lifted Eli's arms, placed them around my neck, and carried her up on my back. The man's hammering stopped. He paused to look at me and swam towards us. I ran to the bushes.

"Wait," Ojosama's weak voice called after me. "How did you find us?"

I paused for a moment. "A friend told me." I ran into the forest, over the downed logs and across the bushes until it was dark enough for nobody to spot us.

CHAPTER THREE

Maya

A RED RIBBON ROSE FROM THE ROCKS AT the bottom of the Anmon River. I looked into the river's silver surface, watching the unfamiliar green eyes that stared back at me. The tattoo on my neck itched. I peered over the stream into the distance where burned twigs lay in a pit on the other end of the river. The current of the water quickened when dawn broke. I traced the shape of a spider on the hilt in the water and recognized it as a kunai from the Mori Clan. I tugged at the thick wire around my ponytail. My hair fell onto my shoulders. I flung away fallen hair strands and promised to never dye my hair again.

I tied the end of the wire through the hole in the

hilt, and loosened a kunai from the bunch that dangled in a chain around my belt. One of my blades had a blunt end. Usually, I sharpened the ends like spears, but this one was stubborn. It looked like the kunai my village used for rice planting.

Many branches of beech trees hung over the water and the bridge of rocks bordered the edge of the Anmon Falls. The rocks became slippery when the current rose, making the fall more dangerous. I tied the end of the wire to the hole in my hilt, identified the spider etched into it like the one in the water, stretched the wire to the lowest tree branch that hung over and stabbed the kunai into the bark. The wire swayed with the tree branch five feet above.

I snapped a long twig from the branch and knocked away the lighter rocks on the top. The water carried them down the Anmon falls. The tide rose.

Come on … Come on!

I waited for the rocks at the bottom to budge. The wind blew in my direction. The water rose higher and higher and higher.

"Yes!" I jumped up to catch the flying blade. I released my kunai from the branch and untied the wire that joined them. They clanked together as I attached them to my belt. The black blade dangled alongside five other silver ones that glimmered from the rising sun's rays.

"He's going to come back, I'm telling you." A girl and a Japanese man approached the pit of burned wood across the river. "He needs his weapon, how else will he survive in this forest?"

I hid behind a tree.

"He saves my life and then steals my badge—"

The Japanese man gestured for the girl to halt.

"What is it, Juro?" she asked him.

Juro lifted the binoculars around his neck to his eyes.

The girl crossed the bridge of rocks and checked the spot where I snatched the blade. "It's gone!"

I lunged over the arched roots of trees, ran, grabbed a branch and swayed over the broken logs—but my sweaty palms slipped. I landed on both feet and leaned against a wide beech tree. My heart throbbed, my face burned and my breath broke out in short gasps. I lost track of my predators and no longer heard them in the distance.

The ground shook. The leaves vibrated. A shadow split from the shade of the trees as a black bird soared over the branches and disappeared south of the river. I glanced around the tree. A pack of grey and white serows charged down. The ground shook as a group of them thundered past and disappeared to my right. I exhaled and peered back to the left. The girl and her guard hid six rows of trees behind.

"We know you're out there!" the girl shouted. "We just want what you took from us." She fumbled for her camera, adjusting its lens.

Something was wrong. I smelled decay. The ground shook more intensely than when the serows had come. Something big was coming.

"Konaide!" I yelled in Japanese. "Stay back!"

"Oh ho, the girl speaks." The girl and the Japanese man moved closer towards my tree. "Just wait till I show this to my viewers. I'm going to be the next Sharon."

"I'm warning you..." I wrapped the wire around my hair several times, tied a knot and rolled up my leather gloves. My exposed fingers loosened all blades from my belt. I gripped three in each hand, each blade clutched between two fingers.

HOOF!

The girl and the Japanese man stepped back. Our heads turned to the left. Bushes and leaves flew from side to side, twigs and wooden chips cracked, more calls from feathered creatures echoed in the sky and the vibrations on the ground quickened with each step. A big black head emerged from the bushes, and with the might of a thousand pounds, the claws of the animal crunched a log.

"Bear!" I shouted. All three of us ran down the serows' tracks. The ground quaked as the black bear chased us.

"How did you know it was coming?" the girl panted as she caught up with me, her camera pointing at her back.

I looked down at the woman's leather boots with two inch flat heels. "That heel's going to break," I snorted. Her left heel broke off and she swayed to one side. I grabbed her arm, pulled her towards me and we both tumbled down the slope of a hill. I pushed the girl off me and rolled over to catch sight of the serows ahead.

"My camera," the girl whined. It had slipped out

of her hand and was nowhere to be found.

"You go straight there and you…" I gestured to the Japanese man at the top of the hill. "Go left." I split from the serows' tracks and headed to the stream.

"W-Wait!" the girl called after me and then turned to follow after the serows' tracks. The black bear sniffed the air and slowed down.

"Over here!" I clanked the blades against each other.

The bear's ears pricked.

I ran to the Anmon Falls and clanked my blades again. The bear charged towards me and I scratched his black fur as he plunged into the water. Blood dripped from my lip. I licked it.

The bear's head erupted from the water and shook as he paddled towards me.

I threw my arms over the tree branch above the river and landed on the line of rocks that bordered the Anmon Falls.

The bear attempted to mount the rocks, but the strength of the current carried his weight closer to the edge of the fall. His forepaws dug into the rocks, causing them to crack. He pulled himself forward as I crossed to the other end of the river. More rocks loosened under the bear's weight. He made a sound like a yelp, before slipping over the edge and dropping down the two-story high waterfall. I peered over the edge. The bear moaned. He paddled away from the waterfall and limped to shore.

"Is it dead?" The girl climbed over the border of rocks behind me.

I pointed my blades at her, like claws.

"Whoa!" The girl raised her hands. "You have so many of them. Are you a Mori?"

I took a step back when she came closer.

"I don't think you want to kill me," the girl said with a smirk. "You just saved us from a bear."

"Drop it." Something touched my back.

"That's Juro. He works for me." The girl pointed to the Japanese man behind me. A silver bracelet glimmered around her wrist. "Isn't it nice to have someone obey your every word? This man will kill you if I tell him to."

"You got ten men keeping you and your pretty clothes from being scathed?" I snickered. "Juro means the tenth man, doesn't it, Lady Aya Hidek—"

"You will address her as Ojosama." Juro's weapon

pushed into my back again and I felt its width.

"You recognize me?" Aya chuckled. "Of course, who wouldn't know the Hideki Group if it wasn't for the Kan—"

I cut the silver bracelet loose from around Aya's wrist, twisted her arm behind her back and raised the bracelet to my teeth. "Hard. The next time I won't go gentle on you." I grinned, pushed her forward and dodged the blow from Juro's stick.

I scratched his chest with my claws. He scampered back in pain.

"Calm down, little girl. We just want to ask you a question." Aya nursed her hand. "Who's your employer?"

I looked down the waterfall at the bear. He growled at my predators from the shore, and tried to climb up the slope. "He's scared of the trick I just pulled on him," I told them. "He might not like it if you get to me first."

Aya backed away from the edge and held on to Juro's shoulder.

"Celio took your badges, I presume?"

Aya and Juro nodded.

"Did you tell your father?"

"If I told him that the last surviving members of the Italian family attacked me," Aya explained, "he might just pay the Kan to orchestrate another fire, even if it were to break out in this forest."

"So, why didn't you?"

"Because that's not how I want to win." She smiled.

"So, just start afresh. Go after your predator." I stepped back onto the soil again. "This bear ran after serows until it found something sweeter. Don't you think?"

"It sounds a lot like something you did to the Kan."

I snapped a twig under my foot and tightened my fingers around the kunai. "I'm not a snake!" I spat. "Not anymore."

"See? We have a lot to talk about."

***

Slash. Slash. I scraped the wood. I let them get to me again. Slash. Slash. I marked three lines with my kunai on the bark of each tree.

My eyes landed on a brown nest in a hornbeam.

I climbed up and reached inside it. "It's still here." Relieved, I pulled my hand back and withdrew an egg to my lips.

Ka kaw … kaw … kaw, the whistle echoed in the forest.

The songs of birds quieted. I counted to three and whistled again.

Ka kaw … kaw … kaw.

I remembered the time when a woman with chestnut hair once asked me if I liked birds. She had a rifle slung across her shoulder and a dead bird tied to her waist. We walked down a yellow forest trail that had a line of budded flowers waiting to bloom.

"Bonjourno," she said to an old farmer pushing a three-wheeled wooden cart past us.

"Bonjourno, Signora," he said, tipping his hat.

"Signora?" I asked.

"The people here are too kind," she said. "Just call me Amelia."

I spotted a treehouse ahead and Amelia led me up the ladder. Drawings and dolls decorated the wooden walls. She walked onto the porch and grabbed a chair. "Come."

I took her hand.

"What do you see?"

I peered into a nest on a branch. "Eggs."

"And?"

"One of them is blue."

"Exactly. Now, keep watching."

Tiny grey arms sprung out from the blue egg as it cracked open. The nestling's beak opened and it let out a cry. With webbed feet, it stepped out of its shell and pecked at the eggs around it. It bent its head crookedly as it pushed the eggs out of the nest, one by one. I watched them splatter on the ground.

"It's a Cuckoo," Amelia said, "in a Dunnock's nest."

"What will the mother do when she comes back?"

"She will raise the Cuckoo as her own. She won't even know what happened." Amelia helped me back down again. "I want you to have this." She handed me an egg-shaped whistle. "I made it for you to always remember who you are and the big future you have ahead of you."

Pushing the memory away, I returned the egg-shaped whistle to the nest, landed on my feet and swirled my blades against the bark of the tree to etch a circle, like a bear marking its territory.

I unrolled a piece of paper from my pocket to reveal a map I had drawn. I pointed at the red mark above where it said Anmon Falls, circled the spot where I found the kunai near the blue line—the Anmon River, drew a spider on the water and turned the paper over. To contestant number one, I read. A list of names written next to badge numbers three, four, five and six marked its corner.

The Kan will know you survived the fire, Aya's voice laughed in my ear. "*Tick-tock. Tick.*"

I tightened the wire around my ponytail, lowered my black hood over my head, erased my tracks and made sure no one followed me. I tucked my hands into my pockets and headed towards the maze of the Nihon Canyon. Climbing the orange and grey walls, I skidded down some rocks that collapsed into the river below. They joined the waterfall over the Shadow Gate, a wall that caved in during an earthquake three hundred years ago. My fingers felt for the holes in the black and orange stones as I walked alongside the ridge. It felt cold. I pressed my back against it. At five meters high, I could see the entire forest including the roof of a five-floored pagoda. The white-peaked mountains surrounded us, the maze unfolded beneath the ridge, a part of it barred by the hunters' fence, and the Mori Mountain spanned the other half of the forest past it. I grasped an opening in the wall behind me and, in the dark, I lead myself into the mouth of a cave.

"The security office lets us bring in weapons, except for matches," a voice echoed from inside.

"Jun?" I crouched near the long-haired assassin, took the stone in his hand and scratched my blunt blade against it. The dead weeds caught fire. Jun's face lightened. His glasses glared.

"New bracelet? Looks expensive."

I rubbed the silver bracelet around my wrist and sneered. "That was fast. Did you catch your—"

"Prey?" another voice replied. A boy with a magenta mohawk smiled—Masaki. His metallic braces reflected orange. "Funny how your team of screwups fell for that American's tricks."

Jun stood up, fists clenched by his sides. "Shima's the idiot, always flashing around his bag of badges. He was bound to get caught."

"And what about you?" Masaki laughed. "You really lost your prey's badge? I mean, what do you expect, coming from a guy who couldn't even take down one of the Triplets."

Jun grabbed Masaki's collar and shoved him against the wall.

"Oi!" I lit a stick on fire and held it up. It caught Jun and Masaki's gaze. "I wonder if anyone would ever find two dead bodies here."

"Don't joke arou— Hey, hey." Masaki backed away when I swung the lighted stick at him. Jun and Masaki's eyes reflected fear.

"Fire is what will keep us alive." I threw the stick into the pit. "You have something for me, Masaki?"

Masaki tossed a pouch at my feet and kicked the rubble. "I hate it when you do that. And take those green contacts off; they remind me of those damn Kan. It wasn't that long ago that you left them."

"I didn't leave them," I said. "Mr. Mori saved me from them." I opened the pouch and dropped four badges on my lap.

Masaki crouched down and lit a cigarette in the fire. "I stole their badges."

"You idiot!" Jun punched Masaki. Masaki's mohawk got squished by his weight against the wall.

"Did any of them follow you? You're going to lead them all here to our hideout!"

"If they do we'll just get rid of them, just like how the owners erased all traces of us. We don't even exist in the system." Masaki flicked the ash from his cigarette and exhaled in Jun's face. "They're the ones who were too stupid to keep their badges on. Unlike Jun, I've got mine hidden somewhere."

"And their prey?" I flipped the badges over and placed them on the rocky ground.

"Shima's taken care of that."

I grabbed the white rock near the fire and scribbled a line through each number on the black wall of the cave. "That makes four down. How many more to go?"

"Are you serious?" Jun interrupted. "I thought you could recognize them, since you've worked with them before."

"They're different each year." I shrugged. "Except for the Triplets. They never age. Hey, Masaki. Who's Minoru's prey?"

"I don't know, man." Masaki scratched his head, keeping the cigarette between his lips. He shivered. "It's not like he tells me anything. You'll have to ask him."

"What you do with the Kan's badge number?" I cocked my head at Jun.

"Same as I do every year. I gave it to Shima to make the exchange with the forager." Jun returned the paper, cranked the lid of his flask open and I waved away his offer for a drink.

"If the Kan make it into the next round, it's going to be hard to track them down," I said. "Not with the Juniko lakes around."

"Well there's five less Kan to worry about." Jun downed a shot of his sake. He always lowered his eyes after a drink, too ashamed of his drinking problem. All those years of hunting had worn him out; the things he'd seen had led him to drinking his pain away. I never saw him smile.

"Five." Badge number ninety clicked against the pile. The three of us looked up. Enura's tall figure stooped over us. He had a cloth with a red stain just below a web that marked his sleeveless arm.

"You okay?" I eyed his wound.

"I'm fine." Enura's low monotone voice echoed in the cave. He held my gaze. "I have some bad news. Shirakawa's alive."

"Shirakawa?" Masaki gulped. "H-how?"

The flask quivered in Jun's hand. "Are you sure?"

"I saw him check in with my own eyes." Enura pointed to his eyes.

"You see this." Masaki lifted the right cover of his jacket to reveal a scar below his shirt. "The guy almost killed me at last year's competition. If he's really alive, we're all screwed."

"I'm telling you, I would've seen him," Jun argued.

"Are you okay?" Enura knelt down beside me.

I nodded as Jun and Masaki got into another one of their brawls again.

"I thought you killed him," Enura said quietly, making sure the rest couldn't hear.

"I pushed him into the flames and watched him burn," I said. "I can still feel the fire."

I can feel it...God, and it's so hot...

I clenched my fists—remembering what it was like. I was in Italy all over again.

"The fire is getting out of control," a Kuma Hunter had informed me. A chandelier crashed behind him, its shards showering us. The Kan had rushed into a hall surrounding a woman holding a whip.

"You're here to take me out too?" She said. "This

is a rescue mission, not an assassination! Stand down."

A gallon rolled into the hall and exploded. We took shelter inside another room, shelves of books burning around us.

"I can't see!" I heard the woman cry from the hall. "Takeshi!"

A man with a spider tattoo on his head lunged at me. "Where are the children?"

"They're all dead," a Kan sneered, bringing his elbow down on the man's back.

"What are you doing?" I shouted.

"The Kan wants everyone dead, including the spiders," the man said, marching into the hall. He aimed his gun at the spiders, gathering around a woman with her eyes on fire.

"Stay with me!" A man with a katana yelled at her, fighting off anyone who dared attack them.

The whimpers of a child jerked my head around. "Mommy," it said. I scanned a fallen shelf with a girl stuck underneath it. I pressed my palms against its burning edges.

"Step back!" a voice behind me snapped.

I reached for a kunai at my side and turned

around. Before I could let go of the hilt, I paused. "Celio?"

"How do you know my name?" the boy said, pointing a bat at me.

"Help me get your sister out." I tossed him the kunai as we both shoved our hands against the shelf. The girl crawled out from underneath and hugged her brother.

"Help!" a man yelled from the hall. Shots fired and shouts followed.

"Run." I pushed the children into a corridor as a pillar detached from the ceiling and fell between us, slamming into the floor and sending up clouds of dust and ash. "Get out of here!"

"What about you?" the boy asked. "Our Parents?"

"I'm sorry," I said. A boulder smacked against the side of my head. I rolled over the ground, blood trickling down my face.

"Get up," a voice demanded.

I looked up to see Shirakawa with long black hair and a bear tooth chained to his neck.

A gentle touch on my shoulder brought me back to the present again.

"He almost killed me," I told Enura in the cave. "I

don't think I can kill him again."

"You won't have to do it alone," he comforted.

Jun surrendered as Masaki let go of his arm behind his back.

"Where's Minoru?" Masaki asked. "He's not going to believe me when I tell him that I took you down."

Jun grabbed Masaki's arms, rolled over and shoved him into the ground. "Never."

"Okay, okay."

Jun let Masaki go. Masaki snatched his flask and was disappointed with the one drop left.

"Minoru is late." Enura eyed his watch.

"He'll be fine," Masaki said. "It may be his first contest, but we all trained him, including his mother. He'll make it on time to his birthday celebration, if that's what you're worried about."

"We'll have to stop the Kan and win the contest if we even want to make it to the party," Jun said, pushing up his glasses.

"I know how we can draw them out," I said. I took a step away from the cave wall. We all stared at my plan. "That should eliminate them from the first round."

"And if they regroup?" Jun asked.

"We'll just draw their blood," Masaki smirked.

"No, we will not start another feud between our clans," I warned. "Just because they keep coming after us, doesn't mean we should too. They're all waiting for us to slip up so they can have a reason to attack. We're going to have to do it quietly."

Masaki dropped the cigarette and stepped on it. "You're starting to sound like our mother," he said. "Just remember, we don't work for you."

"Of course." I smiled, clutching the cool blades by my side.

"We don't make a move until Minoru's dad gives us the go, okay?" Masaki kicked the badges into the flame. The paint peeled off. He stomped on the last bits until everything turned into ash.

CHAPTER FOUR

The Forager

I PUSHED MY LONG BANGS BACK WITH A bandanna. Slapping the dust off my hands, I emptied a water bottle over my fingers, flicked drops into my eyes, and drank the rest. A number of phones scattered at my feet. Not one of them had a signal. An alarm went off in a pink cased phone.

There were two days until the contest ended. I closed the pink flip phone, slipped it into my pocket and rummaged through the bags around me. Muddy footprints covered the ground, but nobody had touched the things in these bags, not for days.

I munched on a pack of sweet and sour Twizzlers and licked one finger after another. The pink phone in my pocket vibrated once, twice and played a tune. I grabbed the worn out guitar from behind me, tightened the knob at the left end, hummed along with the tune and began to pluck the six strings.

"Someday, in the future," I sang in Japanese, "I'll find myself running from the light that shines in your empty heart and sets your soul ablaze. The fireflies have flown off into the summer sky never to return. Hotaru no haka—" The phone stopped ringing. "The grave of the fireflies ..." My finger reached the node where the string no longer hung. It was a broken guitar that nobody wanted. I tossed it back on the ground behind me. The phone vibrated again.

"Who the hell keeps calling?" I opened the flip phone and answered. "What?"

"H-hello?" the voice on the other line said.

"Stop calling!" I hung up. "Stupid phone...only good for receiving calls. What about my phone call?" I yelled at the phone and stretched my arm back to fling it into the nine meter deep Aoike Lake of Juniko.

A man stood ten feet away with a black phone against his ear. He pushed down the antenna. He wore a green helmet, a mix of green, brown and black shades of an army suit and black boots that reached up to his knees. He had a bowie knife strapped to the right boot and was armed from the bulky look of his jacket. No soldier came into this area of the forest on my watch, not for the past ten years.

"Sir, I'm going to have to ask you to give me back that phone."

I looked at my hand in the air and lowered the phone back down. "You don't look English." His black hair and crescent eyes didn't fool me under that helmet.

"Denwa kaerushite kudasai…onegai," the man repeated, in Japanese this time, and turned his palm up.

"No Japanese soldier wears what you're wearing. I can see you tore the ranks off your shoulder." I pointed to the loose ball of string where three or four bands had clearly been ripped off. "In Japan, the soldiers place those on the other shoulder. Are you South Korean?" I took a few steps toward him and felt for the empty patch where his platoon mark should have been. The man pushed my hand away. I snatched the phone from him, ran back to my spot and pulled out the antenna.

"What are you doing?" The soldier tried to take it back. I pushed some buttons as I held my hand up in the air. Circles and squares flashed on the screen. "Oh, you're definitely not Japanese. Chinese Characters is what we use here in Japan, something you Koreans abandoned."

I snatched my other hand away from the soldier's grasp. He stumbled forward. His helmet landed in the mud and, when he tilted his head up, his eyes flared at me.

"Give. It. Back!" The soldier swung his leg behind mine and threw me to the ground. When I got back up on my knees, he grabbed my left arm and twisted it behind my back to push me down again, nose in the mud.

"Oww!" I tilted my head up. "Okay, okay, you can take the phone."

The soldier grabbed the phone, strapped it to his bag, and released my hand from behind my back. He checked my pockets and opened the pink flip phone, pushing several keys that played a different note each time. The soldier hissed under his breath and looked at the black plastic bags over-filled with garbage I had collected. He rummaged through them until a small silver bell chimed when it hit the ground. The soldier lifted it by the string and clutched it against his chest. He sobbed. I raised myself up, picked up the soldier's helmet and wiped the mud from my kneecaps. I unfolded a blade from my sleeve and hid my hand in the helmet, moving swiftly toward the boy.

The soldier kicked the bags in front of him, once, twice and banged his fist into the Oak tree behind him.

"Hey, hey, hey." I ran over to the bags, carefully refilling them with dirty rags and other accessories that people left behind. I decided to pick up my blade again and approached the soldier's back. "These are my life." I lifted the blade in my hand, bringing it closer and closer to his neck. "You can't be breaking them—"

Tears trickled down the soldier's cheeks when he turned to face me. I hid the blade behind my back before he saw it.

"Oh, come on." I stretched my leg over the bags, but slipped over them and fell. I crawled over people's belongings and crouched near the soldier.

"I'm not angry with you. It's okay. There's no need to cry." I moved his wet hair from his forehead, as he flinched away from me with his back against the tree. "What are you? Like twenty-one? Oh, all right, I'll do this one nice favour for you just this once. Okay? One favour. If you give me that phone and walk away, I'll pretend you were never here, yeah?"

I put the helmet back on his head. The soldier didn't budge. "Come on, now, stop crying." I clipped the strap under his chin, eyed the black phone in his bag strap and reached for it.

"Did you see her?" The soldier faced me, wiping his tears with his muddy fingers.

I raised my hand over his phone and grabbed the dirty rag by the tree. "Here." I gave it to him to wipe his face. "Your girlfriend broke up with you or something?"

More tears streamed down the soldier's face. He looked away.

"Ouch." I pushed my bangs up with my left palm. "Well, you're not going to find her here, buddy. People who left their things have been gone for more than a year now."

The soldier opened the pink phone and pushed buttons until a picture flashed on the screen. "This is Soo Hyeon." The soldier smiled weakly. He rubbed away the tears that fell on the phone screen, as though caressing the girl's face. "Soo Hyeon-a, Hotaru no Haka nomu cho-wa-hae. She really loves that Japanese movie."

"Yeah, I know someone who does, too. Argh, you really want to keep that phone, don't you," I groaned.

"Where did you find it?"

I sighed and rubbed my kneecaps again. "I'll show you. If that's what it takes for you to leave." I wrapped an arm around the soldier and helped him up.

We followed the hiking trail of a lake with steam rising from its center. From the tall pines around the lake's circular concave edge came not a sound, no movement of branches, or birds calling. The water was as flat as any mirror except for the steam that rose from the middle.

"What's that?" The soldier pointed to the bubbles rising in the center.

"Welcome to Aoike Lake," I said. "They call it Juni,

as in twelve lakes, but actually—" I pointed to the rail bridge in the distance. "If you follow that path it takes you to all thirty-three of them. It used to be all one big lake three hundred years ago, until an earthquake nearly leveled this entire forest and killed everything inside it. You see, a number of these mountains around us are part of the ring-of-fire. They erupted a long time ago, leaving us with pits like these." I picked up a rock and tossed it into the middle of the lake. "It'll sink for hours, and then it'll melt."

"So, it's a hot spring?" the soldier asked.

"A hot spring?" I laughed. "No, not if you want to boil yourself to death. It's a pit with no end."

The soldier examined fresh footprints in the mud.

"Are you even listening?"

"This belongs to a man." The soldier traced the mud print with his two fingers. "They're coming out of the water."

"That's impossible," I said. "No one can step into this lake."

The soldier pointed in the direction the footprint followed. He crouched over the tall blades of yellow grass, and slowly crept forward until the trail ended. "Do many people come around here?"

"Juniko closed this summer, so not even tourists are allowed in except for me. They leave it up to me to clean up—" I turned to the transparent crystal blue water of Aoike Lake. It mirrored my surprised face.

I said too much.

Long and uncombed hair hung over my face. The tips touched my shoulders. Some of the strands covered the scar beneath my eye, but the light reflected in the water exposed its faint yellow color. A white, grey and yellow spotted Ayu fish split my reflection as it swam by. They only lived in the forest for a year and this one was going to die soon. Newborns hatched yellow and turned white and grey when approaching death. In a way, we were alike, and not just because of my greying-white hair.

"Who's they?"

I turned away from the Ayu fish. "The owners— who are going to be angry with me when they find out you're here. Now, let's go find your girlfriend and send you two home before dark." I climbed over the slope and showed the soldier how to grab onto the branches that sprouted from the ground.

At the top of the slope, we reached the rails of the bridge made out of rope. The bridge swayed when we stepped on it. The clear cerulean water tinged with green brightened under the sunlight like opals. At the center of the bridge, it looked as though we walked on green Beech and Oak trees rather than the blue sky. Aoike Lake mirrored things at different angles depending on the weather or season.

When we crossed to the other slope, the color of the water changed back to a gradient purple and continued to change when viewed from various points along the hiking trail. We reached the spring water of Wakitsubo, another lake that was part of Juniko. Wakitsubo Lake flowed through Virgin Beech forests and down the side of the steps. I planted my leg over the stones that reached the center of the stream where the statue of a Buddha prayed. I picked up a white stone cup from the base.

"This flows straight from Wakitsubo Lake," I explained to the soldier as I lowered the cup into the stream. "It contains various minerals. Even doctors use it to make medicines." I took a sip and passed it over to the soldier. He sniffed it, cringed and tilted his head away.

"Come on." I pushed the cup closer to his mouth until I made sure he drained it. "That a boy."

I plucked the white Mantema flowers that grew on the wet stones and tucked them in my pocket. We turned away from the stream and hiked down the other side of the slope. The soldier grasped the tree branches, as I had shown him. A fast-learner. "Is your military training off the coast of Korea?"

The soldier didn't reply.

"You know I could ask you a lot of questions, like did you run away from a marine base, make your way over to the west coast of Aomori? It would explain why you tore off your bands. But I guess you're not going to answer any of them."

The soldier halted behind a tree.

"So, you did abandon your service?"

"Shh…" The soldier held a finger to his lips.

"Ok, I'm sorry I asked. You're quite sensitive for a soldier—"

I looked over the branch and saw a boy with spiky purple hair at the bottom of the slope. "Oh no." I joined the soldier behind the tree. "Stay here."

The boy tightened an elastic band around his arm and stabbed himself with a needle. He stared into the water, spat, and adjusted his lip piercing. A chain hung from it and went down his chin to the chain around his neck.

"Masaki," I whispered. "He's doing that stuff again."

"Who—"

I shushed the soldier, took a deep breath, and scanned the fenced premises. "If you see any black birds in the sky, duck." I marched out of my hiding.

"Masaki," I waved. "What a surprise. You've come to visit."

"Urusai, Ossan," Masaki swore and spat again into the water. "Shut up, old man. You talk too much, eat too much, sleep too much—what is that smell?" Masaki's nose cringed when I got closer. He loosened the elastic around his arm, and brought it to his pocket.

"What are you doing here, Masaki?" I pulled on his wrist and found the needle in his palm. "This again?"

"Urusai, Ossan," Masaki spat again.

I grabbed his chin and watched his pupils dilate. "You know that stuff's going to kill you if you keep it up."

"I need it." Masaki pulled back.

"That's what all druggies say." I released my hold of him.

"I'm not a druggie."

"Okay, but spider venom can be addicting."

Masaki grabbed onto my collar and stared into my eyes. "If I'm going to make it out of here alive, I need it." He let go of my collar and straightened my shirt. "Now, did you finish cleaning up?" Masaki scratched his arms. He had goosebumps everywhere and his hair was on end. "Our winners will be coming here soon and we don't want leftovers from last year's winners lying around."

"They're all packed in bags and ready to be exhumed at the temple."

"Excellent!" Masaki smirked. "The Kan will get what's coming to them." A twig snapped and Masaki's head jerked up towards the slope. "Who's there?"

I grasped Masaki's shoulder. "Just an animal."

"Don't play jokes with me, Ossan." He marched

by the fence and to the slope, taking a cigarette out.

"You can't be smoking that near the trees." I followed after Masaki.

"Urusai." Masaki pushed me back. "I know there's someone up there. Who are you trying to hide, huh?" He put the cigarette between his lips, loosened the chains around his wrists and tightened them with both hands.

"Okay, okay, I admit." I held both hands up in the air. "I caught a Japanese hare for dinner."

Masaki laughed. "So all that fuss about being a vegetarian was a lie? Wait till Mother hears this; she's going to kill you! You can't be eating those engineered animals."

"I know, I know. So please don't tell her." I turned Masaki around to Aoike Lake.

Another twig snapped and wooden shavings rolled down the slope. Masaki looked back at the tree on the slope. A branch broke off. The soldier tumbled down with it. As soon as he landed on his feet, he sprung out of his spot and clasped on to the handle of his K2 rifle.

The cigarette fell out of Masaki's mouth.

"You brought a soldier into the forest?!" he yelled.

"No, no, no, he's a friend." I crossed both hands over each other several times to explain to the soldier. "He's not going to harm you."

"I can't believe you brought a soldier into the forest!" Masaki loosened a kunai from the chain around his wrists and flicked it open in his right hand. "Stay back, Ossan."

"Oh, like a knife is going to do anything," I mocked, as I took a step closer to the soldier. "Calm down, sunny, he's just a friend. He's going to help us find Soo Hyeon. Remember? Soo Hyeon."

"Soo Hyeon?" the soldier asked.

"Who the hell is Soo Hyeon?" Masaki spun the blade on the end of his chain. His head spun in all directions, and his dilated eyes searched for anyone or anything to attack. "Do I have to kill her too?"

The soldier aimed his rifle at Masaki.

"No, no, no." I stood between them. "No one's going to kill anybody. I told you, we're going to help you."

"Who's going to help him?" Masaki yelled. "Me? Ossan, you have lost your mind. Do I need to kill you, too?"

"Shut up, Masaki," I snapped back at him. "That's the venom talking. I'm trying to calm him down, and you're about to get us all killed."

"Soo Hyeon?" the soldier asked again.

"Yes, yes," I nodded. "The girl with the long black hair." I gestured over my head. "Now put the gun down and come over here slowly."

The soldier hesitated and nodded toward Masaki's spinning blade.

"Where is she?" Masaki yelled hysterically.

"Put the blade down, Masaki."

"Shiksho."

"Masaki, put the blade down."

Masaki released the chain and the blade struck the ground. "This is all your fault, old man. You and your god damn hare. Vegetarian? Pfft." Masaki spat.

"I can get rid of that for you. The taste of metal. It's a side effect of the drug."

Masaki unclipped his blade from the chain.

The soldier lowered his gun and approached us slowly.

"See? That wasn't so bad." I turned to the soldier.

Masaki sprinted over to the soldier and punched him to the ground.

"You little—"

"Hey!" I caught Masaki's fist. "He's got a military phone on him and those things come with a tracker. What if his platoon comes looking for him? We can't have his dead body lying around here."

"Who are you?" Masaki clutched onto the soldier's collar, yanked him up and then threw him to the ground again.

I grabbed the soldier's arm, helped him to his feet and slapped the dust off him.

"What are we going to do?" Masaki paced back and forth. "We are so screwed!"

"He's looking for his girlfriend," I told Masaki. "Once he finds her, he'll be on his way. It's no big deal."

"You've got to be kidding me! Listen, Ossan, I had no part in this, okay?! There's so much time left before the round is over and this place better be cleared out before then ... including him! I don't care where he's from or why he's here. There better not be any more soldiers like him trespassing like this, or I'm going to personally end you!" Masaki shoved me with his shoulder and climbed over the fence. When he was no longer in sight, I bent down to pick up the soldier's rifle, strapped it around my shoulder and packed his bag.

"You have to get out of here." I searched the ground for anything else.

"Soo Hyeon?"

"There is no Soo Hyeon, okay?" I yelled at the soldier. "Go back to your country!"

"No!" The soldier remained still. "I-I can't go back. I ran away from my service. You know what happens to South Korean soldiers who run away? They get sentenced for a life time in prison... e-even death."

"Well, it's your fault you came here."

"Please, I have to find Soo Hyeon." The soldier took out a GPS from his backpack where red dots blinked on the map. "These are the places she visited in the past year."

"Listen bud, she probably just left you, okay? Just move on, there's nobody here except her cell phone—doesn't mean it was her who visited all these places. Things get moved around a lot."

"No, that's not true. Soo Hyeon would never leave me. After I got called in for my service, Soo Hyeon had to find a job. We were supposed to get married." The soldier grabbed my shoulders. "When she found out how much money the winners of the contest are awarded, she took a boat here from South Korea last year and—"

"Wait, your girlfriend was a contestant?"

The soldier nodded. "I only found out recently that her parents have been looking for her for the past year."

"I should've known." I slapped my forehead continuously and walked past him. "You idiot, how are you going to explain this to him? That his girlfriend might be dead?" I turned back to the soldier. "Look, uhh … what's your name?"

"Tae Won," the soldier replied.

"I don't think we'll be able to find your girlfriend. All the winners from last year either disappeared or …"

"Or what?" Tae Won shook me by the shoulders.

"Or … I'll tell you what, why don't you join the contest yourself and see where the M— I mean the owners take the winners after?" I rummaged through my jacket pockets. "Here." I handed him two badges, pulled out a yellow sticky note and scribbled a number. "At least now you don't look like you trespassed. You are going to have to give me something else in return."

I took the black phone from the bag and kissed it. "Yes! I can finally have my phone call. Where are you going? You can't join the game looking like that." I gestured for Tae Won to come back, took off my jacket, pants and boots and handed them over. "Now give me your clothes ... and your backpack ... no, I won't touch the things inside, I promise. Now give it to me ... that a boy."

Tae Won held onto his rifle tightly. "You can pick it up after the contest is over. I promise. It'll be just over the bridge."

Tae Won nodded and handed over his military clothes. He follow the path Masaki disappeared in.

On the way back, I found a footprint similar to the one Tae Won and I found on the other side of the lake. The front sole of the print pointed to the water of Aoike Lake. The one on the other side of the lake had the heel coming out of the water.

Did someone walk in and out of this lake?

I pushed the thought away. The Mori children always played around here anyway. I stared into Aoike Lake. I couldn't see my reflection, not from this end.

I climbed the slope to the bridge, crossed to the other side where the garbage bags lay, hauled them over my back and headed home. Two large red pillars of Cypress wood stood on opposite ends of the tori gate. A black rectangular head board connected them at the roof. A shimenawa rope stretched from corner to corner of the roof holding a picture of a white God in the center—a Shirakami.

I followed the dry path under the gate and headed to the wooden steps that led to the main hall of the square shaped temple. Four red pillars on each corner supported the black-shingled roof. I kicked the screen door to the side, dropped the bags on the matted floor, sat down with my back facing them and untied my muddy black boots to keep them outside.

A light turned on in the hall, the heavy scent of incense flooded my nose, and I rose to my feet. A tall white man with wet blonde hair stood in front of the hearth, holding one of my matches.

"Who are you?"

"I came to see the forager." The white man dropped something onto the center of the table.

The light went out and the man lit another match. I peered under the light and saw American dollar bills held together with an elastic band.

"Now where's badge number nine?"

CHAPTER FIVE

Nick

A CLOCK TICKED BEHIND ME. I TRIED TO GET UP, only to be pulled down by cuff links that shackled my hands to a table. Grey concrete walls caved in on me. There was nothing but a locked door and a black window. A man, with a shirt buttoned tightly around his belly, walked in with a stack of files tucked under his arm.

"Good, you're awake," he said.

Flashing colors blinded me and my head throbbed around my skull.

"You really know how to take a hit, don't you?" the man said.

"Captain?" I squinted from the fluorescent lights. I felt like someone had bashed my head in.

"I'm not your captain anymore, Nick." He sighed. "It's over." He opened the files onto the table to reveal a lawsuit. "I warned you, Nick. I told you to stay away from the big fish. These people are going to keep coming after you until you're dead."

"On what charge?" I yelled.

"You name it. Trespassing, defamation, even felony." The captain spread out the pictures in front of me. Each one had depicted a crash, one in the surveillance room, another in the labs. "Now, are you going to tell me that that's not you?" The captain tapped his fingers against the last picture.

I saw my face in the corner of it and squeezed my eyes shut.

"Get him some coffee, will you?" The captain knocked on the window.

"I heard someone call for help," I said.

"Yeah, yeah, we checked the entire premises, there was no one there."

I cleared the table with both hands, banging my fists down. "No! They're lying! They're not just a biotech company, the experiments, the bio-weapons…they call themselves the Kan! I got it all at my place. Just take a look."

"Already did, Nick. We got nothing. You got nothing. As far as we know,"—the captain pointed a thumb at the window behind him—"you're making it all up. I understand, Nick. You want their attention to be on the screens, watching the crowd's praise. You want to be America's hero who saves the day. We all do. But not this time."

"What's it going to take to drop the charges?"

"You drop your case against them—"

"No, you don't understand—"

"No, Nick. You don't understand. It's over. I'm going to need your badge and your gun."

***

Beep. Beep. The cab honked in the middle of New York City's busiest street.

"I'll get out here." I dropped ten bucks onto the passenger seat, opened the door, and hit the car next to me. "Sorry." I waved, coffee in hand, and crammed myself out the small space. The sun scorched down my back as I crossed onto the sidewalk and headed into a ten-story building.

"Nick, Nick." A man in a suit and tie stopped me

at the door. "You can't be here."

"I'm here to get my stuff, Jim."

Jim blocked my way into the elevator. "Don't."

"Sorry." I kneed him in the stomach and shoved past him into the elevator.

"I need all men on guard," Jim ordered into his receiver.

I tapped the button furiously as the doors closed. My hand instinctively reached for my waist. "Crap." I loosened a metal bar from the wall of the elevator and hid by the door. The elevator opened and two men scuttled in. When they turned, I jammed the bar into one's face and knocked out a gun from another. The bar cracked down on one's shoulder and he crashed into the other. I slipped between doorways and corners, finally reaching my corridor. An armed man in a suit guarded the door to my apartment. I pulled one of the men's receivers to my mouth. "One man down. I repeat: one man down."

The man at the door picked up the signal and scurried down the corridor past me.

I dashed into my apartment. It had been torn apart from corner to corner. Boxes were emptied out on the floor, and the wind from the window blew papers into a pile. I pulled down the yellow tape and turned down a hall to my bedroom. My wall had been punched in, leaving a pin board hanging on one angle. All my research was gone. The captain was right. I stepped into a pile of clippings. One caught my eye. A giant smile was plastered on a girl's freckled face as she stood in a forest holding a check. The header read: "We have a winner."

***

Silvery rays penetrated the dense canopy above. Birdsong came in lulls and bursts, and my fingers came away dry from the soft and damp moss beneath me. The water flowed quietly and black trunks against a bluish charcoal sky surrounded me. I pulled myself up. The path I was once on had become a deep brown. I rapidly breathed in the cool air and my head throbbed. I rubbed the back of my head to find dried blood on my fingers and jerked around to the tree and wires hanging from a branch.

He was gone.

Darkness pressed in on me from all sides. He must have somehow cut himself loose and knocked me out with a rock. Muffled sounds came in from a distance. I searched the black ground and came across my bag, pulling out a receiver.

A number of voices spoke in Japanese, tuning in and out.

"Subete Juniko ni kuru," a voice ordered.

"Shima," I whispered. I shoved my things into my bag and headed towards the sound of the river. Taking a few gulps, I saw an orange glow from within the trees and smelled smoke. I came across a narrow path down a hill, uneven by knotted roots. Songs and cheers permeated from the trees. A twig snapped under my foot and a strap wrapped around my ankle. I bent down to find a camera.

"Yes," I whispered, turning it on. A video started playing on the screen and I let the LED light shine the way through the forested path. A girl with long black hair appeared on the screen. She talked into the camera and then turned it to show an older man with a scruff. He sat on a couch with a newspaper in hand.

"Oto-san," she said. The man looked up and smiled at the camera. They exchanged with each other in Japanese, and the girl kissed her father on his cheek. The video skipped to the girl in a helicopter talking to the camera. She jumped out the door, a man strapped behind her. She dropped through the air with the camera shaking as snippets of the forest and the mountains came into view. The video cut out when they landed and skipped to the line-up at the base. I let it play while I used the light to take my steps carefully. The orange glow in the distance got bigger and bigger.

"Welcome to the Shirakami-Sanchi forest," the voice said. I looked at the video to see the girl standing in front of a familiar backdrop. "It's known as Japan's White-God Mountain or, as I like to call it, the place where you come to die." She laughed. "Ok, let me try again. Scan lines cut through the video. "Welcome to the Shirakami-Sanchi forest."

"Welcome, brother," a voice hissed at me in the dark. I pointed the camera up to find a man peering down at me. He grabbed me by the shoulders and pulled me into an open area by a bonfire.

"Hey!" A crowd cheered as I stumbled in.

"Come, come and join us." A man with broad shoulders and arms as thick as a boulder, ushered me closer.

"Oh-kay?" I shut off the camera and tucked it into my bag. "What's going on here?"

"It's Iyomante," he said. "The sacrifice for the Gods!"

I felt the air lodge into my throat. I watched people huddle around the bonfire, singing and biting meat off bones.

"You hungry?" the man asked. He brought a bone close to my face. I grabbed it and bit into the chunk of meat.

"He-hey!" the crowd cheered.

I held the bone up in the air. "Th-thanks." I grabbed a seat next to a woman on a log.

"I'm Tami." She shook my hand.

"Nick." I swallowed. "This is really good, what is it?"

"Kuma," she said. "Uh…bear."

I choked. A man passed by and I lowered the bone into his plate.

Tami laughed. "Is this your first time in Japan?"

I nodded. The man with broad shoulders grabbed the head of the bear and raised it above his head.

"Rawr!" he shouted to his friends. They all laughed.

"That's Goro," Tami said. "He likes to be called the leader around here."

"And what do you call him?"

"My brother."

"Tami." A man approached with a rifle slung around his shoulder. He had a receiver strapped to his chest.

"Shinriki?" Tami embraced him. They held each other's banded hands.

"It's Keitaro," Shinriki said.

"Stay here." Tami turned to me. She walked over to a tree where a man lay on the ground, and pressed two fingers against his neck. "Goro, I need some help over here."

Goro put down the bear head and gestured for another man to come with him. They lifted the body on the ground and brought him closer to the fire.

"You made it, Keitaro!" Goro cheered. Keitaro

gave them a weak smile as he lay by the fire.

"Hardly," Tami warned. "He shouldn't have jumped over that fence and forced his way in."

"Yeah, but we had your husband to thank." Goro nodded to Shinriki.

My eyes landed on his hunting gear. "You're a Kuma Hunter."

"Yes, he is," Tami answered. She lifted Keitaro's legs onto a log, pulled out a pocket knife, and cut his shirt open. Rashes and bumps crowded his chest. "When did you get bit?" Tami slapped Keitaro awake.

"What happened to him?" I asked Goro.

"It's the wasps. They're massive and pack a deadly punch here. See that guy over there?" Goro pointed to a young man with a vest. "He lost a finger."

Keitaro yelped as Tami smudged berries on his chest.

"How'd you manage to sneak him into the contest?" I asked Goro.

"Tami's husband helps a lot around here." Goro tapped Shinriki on his broad back. "He's our eyes."

"Are you all this big around here?" I asked. "It's just

cause you're all about the same size, dark-skinned, and look very different from Japanese people."

"We're the Ainu tribe." Goro spread his hands up in the air. "This country was our home."

"Until they took it from us," Shinriki added.

"Who? Was it the Kan?" I pulled out a clipping from my bag. "Was it them?" I pointed to a picture of a woman with short brown curls and her team of scientists. They stood in front of a building with a blue and red logo. It looked like the yin and yang except the two sides were divided.

"We don't talk about the Kan," Goro warned. A few repeated after Goro. Then they all broke into laughter.

"Do you know a man named Shima?" I asked.

Goro took a sip of his drink and spat. A few joined in.

"Okay, I take it you're not a fan of the guy."

"We don't talk about him either," Goro slammed his drink into the ground. "One more round, all on me," he announced to the crowd. They all raised their drinks in the air and chanted a song together.

I pressed a finger to my temple. "I guess there are a lot of things you don't like to talk about."

"Shima abandoned our Commune a few years ago," Tami said, rising from Keitaro's bedside. She planted a kiss on her husband's cheek and held his hands. "Be careful," she said to him as he headed back into the forest. "He works for the owners now, just like Shima, except Shima always wanted more than everyone's share. He got greedy and lost his way. We don't live like that here in the Commune. We like to share everything."

"Spend the night here," Goro said. "Fire is what keeps us alive. It keeps what's out there, out there. Look what happened to Keitaro." Goro handed Keitaro a drink.

"I …"

"Take a look around you, there's nothing to see. You're not going to find anything or anyone out here in the dark."

Tami tossed a blanket on me. "Welcome to the Commune," she said.

When the singing died down, I fell into a deep sleep. I didn't wake up until cold hands wrapped around my face.

"Nick."

I shuffled under the blanket, opened my eyes to

meet Tami's and jerked up. "What ... what's wrong?" I looked around.

"Shh ..." She pressed a finger to her lips. I couldn't help but overhear from the receiver." She handed it to me. "You're looking for Shima, right? They said they were meeting with someone named the forager? They're going to be at Aoike Lake, just over the fence near the first base."

"When?" I pulled off my shirt and grabbed a clean one from my bag.

"A few minutes ago." Tami averted her eyes. "I found this in one of the kits." She handed me a flashlight.

"Are you sure?" I took it. "Don't you need it?"

"We'll be fine. There's eleven of us now. We've got more than enough."

I looked at Keitaro passed out near me. I couldn't tell if it was the berries that stained his skin, or if they were bruises.

"He'll be fine." Tami grabbed my hand. "Take care of yourself, brother. And think about it."

"About what?"

"Coming back to the Commune. We're all family here. We can protect you."

"Thanks." I waved. "Don't wait on me." As soon as I was out of sight, I cracked open the camera lens and removed the filter. I cut out pieces of duct tape from my kit and taped the filter to the flashlight. The light dimmed and it was no longer visible. I shoved a paper under my shirt and aimed the torch at it. I pressed record on the camera, and played back the video. It showed the infrared light coming from the torch, exposing the writing on the paper through my shirt. I had built myself an infrared x-ray camera. Using it to see in the dark, I followed a path back to the base. Some contestants had already gathered there, waiting. I slipped from tree to tree and reached the fence. It ran through a lake down a hill. I made my way down and heard a few voices. I shut off the receiver at my side and crept up to the fence. I focused the camera in the dark and saw white figures on the screen.

I checked the camera to make sure it was picking up their voices. A white figure held up a bag and tossed it to a long-haired man. The long-haired men drew an envelope out of his pocket and tossed it to Shima. Shima opened the envelope and counted the bills inside. Shima and his men retreated, laughing and huddling together. I hid behind the vines hanging over the fence until they left. I climbed over and followed the forager in the dark. A red light flashed on the camera and it died. I was surrounded by darkness again.

"No," I hissed, slapping the camera. I pulled out a battery from the flap. It was lithium. There was nothing around here to charge something like that. I ran after the man, helplessly looking for him and I stepped into the blackness of a lake. The water reflected the light sky and my eyes traced the end of it. I walked into the lake, its water rising up to my thigh. The air was pungent with the smell of dead fish. My foot got caught in the mud. I looked down and kicked until a sharp pain pierced down my leg as I freed myself. The water swirled around me and I ran to the other side of the lake as faint rays of morning light seeped in and lit up an open green space in front of me.

I ripped the sleeve of my shirt and wrapped it around the gash on my leg. I looked back at the water but it was still again with steam rising from its center. I limped past the neglected bonsai trees that lined the unshaved lawn, fish swam in a pond under a torn down wooden bridge that crossed the middle, and a riot of flower beds of many colors grew among the weeds. I followed a stone path interrupted by weeds, some overshadowed by fallen down branches that flowed down onto the dank, squishy and mossy ground, its yellowing greens marking the coming season.

A pillared gate stood ahead and I heaved myself onto a wooden veranda under a curved roof. The smell of incense hit me. I slid open a paper-thin door and walked into a hall divided by movable paper walls. Ornaments decorated an altar in a corner. A statue of Buddha sat in its center. I crouched down and picked up a book with a spider logo on its front cover, and pulled on a bookmark that opened to a page filled with drawings of samurai battling against an army. I followed the Japanese characters, even though I couldn't read them. I picked up a box of matches from the altar and slipped into a much smaller hall furnished with a tea table, bags of garbage, a fire place, and some cushions. A light flicked on and a man, with curly black and white hair held back with a bandanna, walked in. I lit a match.

"Who are you?"

"I came to see the one they call the forager." I dropped a bundle of American bills onto the table. The forager peered under the light and saw the money held together with an elastic band.

"Now where's badge number nine?" I asked, taking note of the forager's military clothes.

"How did you find me?" the forager in army clothes asked.

"I saw you meet up with Shima. Four-eyes gave him badge number nine and he gave it you."

The forager looked at me with a blank stare.

"Do you need me to translate that for you?"

"I understand what you said," the forager interrupted. "But what makes you think I still have badge number nine?"

I reached for the dollar bills, but the forager beat me to it. He held them under his nose and smelled it. "You'd be smart enough not to come here unarmed. Too bad this money is mine now."

"Not so fast." I lit another match. "Most houses in Japan burn quite easily." I rested my palm on the wall paper. "So you better hand over the badge before I light this house on fire."

"This is a Zen temple! It's sacred grounds." The forager tossed the money back at me. "Take it and go. I don't have your badge. I threw it into the lake."

Something about the man's voice made me think he was lying. Sweat trickled down my forehead and I dropped down to one knee. I hissed in pain.

"What, what's wrong?" The forager's voice rang in my ears. He peeled off the wet fabric from my leg to reveal a bloody gash that ran down the side of my calf. I struggled to keep my eyes open as I felt heat cloud up my face. My back fell against the cool flat surface of the bamboo mats and my head tilted to the ceiling.

The match went out.

CHAPTER SIX

Celio

A HIGH CHAIN-LINK FENCE SEPARATED part of the forest ahead. A Kuma Hunter, resting a hand on his rifle, paced back and forth.

"You think we can climb over that?" Eli asked.

I checked my bag. "I still have enough arrows. So even if we come across bears on the other side, assuming that's what the fence is for, then we'll be fine."

"Even after you get past the hunter over there?" Eli pointed at the Kuma Hunter with a quivering hand.

I smiled. "I don't need my arrows for that."

We headed down the hill and up to the Kuma Hunter guarding the door.

"You can't be here," he said.

I noticed a wedding band on the hunter's finger.

"Married, huh?"

The Kuma Hunter hid his hand and looked around. "You better leave while you still can."

"You see, that's exactly what we're trying to do," I said. "We want to get over there."

"You can't."

"Why not?"

"Because I said so." The hunter clenched his teeth and pulled his rifle up to his chest.

"Look, if you wanted to shoot us, you would've done so by now." I put my hands up. "But I'm sure if you had kids of your own one day, you'd let them through."

The hunter didn't budge.

I walked around him and pulled onto the fence.

"I did have a daughter," the Kuma Hunter said. "She was just like you."

"That's great, if you let us make it out of here alive, we'll get to meet her."

"She too made it into the next round."

"Oh."

"Where I come from, we live in a Commune."

I sighed and let go of the fence. This was going to be a long story.

"We Ainu have always kept to ourselves, living in the villages, protecting our tribe from the bears. We didn't always live in the North. After the Second World War, the Japanese pushed us out of our homes and drove us up here. We have no choice but to survive. Either fight against our own people, or the bears. I guess you can tell what we chose to do instead. Bears are easier to deal with than people."

"So then, why come here?" I gestured for Eli behind my back to sneak up to the fence. She tip-toed behind the hunter.

"Aomori has been our home since the war until ten years ago."

"When the contests started?"

"Yes, they used the fences to divide us, and now our homes are being taken away from us again."

"What happened to your daughter after the second round?"

"You see that?" he said, pointing to the eaves of a tower. "She died in there. No one ever makes it out of the pagoda, just as you won't make it out of the first."

My eyes widened and Eli froze.

"The only way out is through the front door," the Kuma Hunter turned to Eli. "I have access to it, if you want to leave."

A black bird soared in the sky.

"Duck," the hunter urged. He grabbed us by the hands and pulled us under the shade of a tree. "There are eyes everywhere. If you want to leave, we'll have to do it tonight. It's the only way."

"We don't want to leave," I said. "We want to win."

"Celio," Eli interrupted. "His daughter died, and I-I don't want that to happen to us…"

"Don't talk like that," I cut in. I grabbed Eli by the shoulders and ushered her away from the hunter. "We came a long way. We're so close to getting the answers we need to figure out what happened to our family, to avenge them."

"But I don't want to lose you," Eli whimpered.

"You're not going to lose me. We're going to find help soon. Just trust me, okay?"

"Why can't we just forget the past, it's not like this will bring back mom or dad."

"I know, but I can't live not knowing the truth." I looked back at the hunter as he rubbed his ring finger. "He seems like a good man. If you want to go with him, y-you can."

"No, I won't leave you." Eli grabbed my hand. "If you're going to do this, we'll do it together and if we're going to die, w-we'll die together too."

"I'll be here if you change your mind," the hunter said, going back to his post. "Remember, the forest has eyes. Don't trust anyone."

Eli and I walked along the fence. Every now and then I took out my map to add the distance. I wanted to know how big the first base was. We reached orange and black walls that folded in on each other, like a canyon. We walked through one of the ridges that led to a mountain.

"Halt," a voice echoed.

I grasped my arrow just as a wire wrapped around the bow in my other hand and flung it away.

"Hey!" I yelled. "Show yourself."

A man jumped from the ridge and landed in front of us. He had a bandage around his arm and a tattoo under it.

"Who are you?" I asked.

"I could ask you the same thing." The man circled us.

"Enura, cut it out," a figure landed behind us. Eli

and I turned to see a ponytailed girl.

"You!"

"Catch," she said, tossing me a glimmering blade. I caught it with both hands. It was the kunai I left behind. "H-how did you—"

"You know these kids?" Enura asked the ponytailed girl.

"You could say that," she grinned. "What are you doing here?"

"Looking for you," I stuttered.

"You got a place to stay tonight?"

"Uhh…no."

"Good. Follow me." She walked down the ridge as Enura eyed us. I picked up my bow, tightened my hold on Eli's hand and kept her at my side.

The ridge stretched on for miles. Enura and the ponytailed girl talked in Japanese the whole time. They glanced back at us every few minutes. Enura had a fork attached to a rope at his side. He tossed it up to the ridge and pulled.

"Come on," he said, extending a hand.

I pushed Eli toward him to take it. He pulled her up first and bent down to help me.

"I got it, thanks." I wrapped the rope around

my hand and scrambled up to the ridge. My foot slipped off the edge and Enura caught my hand. He tugged on the rope and hauled me over. "I said I got it."

Enura let go of the rope and I landed on my bottom. "Sure," he said.

"Be nice," Eli whispered.

I rolled my eyes. "Why'd you bring us here?"

"You can spend the night here." The girl showed us into the cave. "No one knows about this place, except for us."

"Who's us?"

Enura whispered into the girl's ear before she could answer.

"Stop bickering around and tell us the truth."

The girl squeezed Enura's hand and came closer to me. I backed up into the wall.

"I'll tell you everything you want to know," she said. "Promise."

"I'll let you catch up," Enura said. "I can be your lookout, you know, in case the rest decide to come here."

"Thanks, Enura," the girl smiled at him. Enura turned away and sat down on the edge.

"I hate that guy," I said.

The girl laughed. "Oh, you haven't changed."

"How do you know me?"

"I know you too, Eli." The girl patted Eli's head. "You guys hungry?" She opened a lunch box and the smell of meat filled the air. "Here." She placed the box on my lap and put chopsticks in my hand.

"How'd you know?"

"I know everything about you."

The chopsticks wiggled in my hand.

"Oh yes, I forgot." The girl took the chopsticks from my hand, plucked a chunk of meat off the box, and brought it close to my mouth. An old memory of the girl dawned on me. She had pressed a hand on my chin and fed me porridge many years ago.

"Say ah," she had said.

"The kids seem to like you a lot." Mom had walked into the kitchen. "They never eat from my hands like they do with you. What's your secret?"

"I just bring my face close like this." The girl stared into my eyes.

"Oh, stop, you're going to give them a scare." Mom laughed.

I pushed away at the thought of the girl ever

being part of my childhood. "You were there the whole time …" I mumbled. "How come I don't remember you?"

The girl pinched her eyes and held her contacts in her hand. "I'm different now." A weak smile spread across her face. "It's been a long time since. You were just ten when I left."

"But you came back, you saved us."

"I failed." The girl lowered her eyes. "I made your mom a promise, to protect you. It all started seven years ago, when the Kan were appointed with running the Mori Group branch in America."

***

"We should have been the ones to go there," Amelia said to her husband, Lorenzo, one night.

"I was just passing by," the girl explained to us, "when I overheard them say …"

"They're going to use it against us. Makoto shouldn't have trusted them. Just because they act under one company doesn't mean they're really on the same side. I can't believe she picked them over us. I won't let her get away with it that easy."

"Dear, we can't pull out now. It's too dangerous, our children are too young," Lorenzo said, gripping Amelia's shoulders. They looked at the files on a table in front of them. "We can't use this." He picked them up and tossed them into the burning fire in the living room. "We need to burn all traces of us working against them. They'll come after us, take away our inheritance, our company, our shares. We can't let them do that. We have no choice but to comply."

"I can help," the girl said, coming out of her hiding. "Take me there. I'll live with them, and take them down from the inside. I can be your eyes, like that bird."

"She's right," Amelia sighed. "It's time."

"It's too dangerous," Lorenzo disputed.

"It's what you've trained me for," I said. "They'll raise me like their own. They won't even notice. Use me."

Amelia hugged the girl. "We took you in as our own," she said. "You were just a little girl left at our door step, all alone and scared. Now, you're almost an adult; you're old enough to make your own decisions. If this is really what you want, fine, but remember, we're your real family. Whatever the Kan tell you or try to do to you, they will never be your family."

"Are you sure? We can talk about this." Lorenzo caressed the girl's shoulder. I nodded and he hugged me. "A plane with our employees is taking off to New York tonight. You'll have to go with them."

"Will I get a chance to say goodbye?" the girl said.

"There's no time," Lorenzo urged. "We should go now if we want this to work."

The girl peered into the dining room as she watched the two children eat and play with their food. Lorenzo placed a hand on her shoulder and they disappeared down a corridor.

***

"For five years I was training with the Kan," the girl continued. "Studying their ways, watching them run experiments on people. The Mori knew about them, but they wouldn't act. They were too concerned with starting another war, and they didn't want their company to suffer. Their reputation was at risk, but so were the lives of many. When I came to tell your parents, they were outraged. What started as a biotech company became a lab that turned people into monsters. They wanted to pull out. It wasn't until a few months ago that the Mori decided to send your family a warning. It was the only way for the Kan to take your inheritance, and to run your family's company in Italy."

I flipped the lunch box over and closed my hands around the girl's throat. "You knew this whole time?!"

"Celio!" Eli apprehended me. "Let her go."

Enura hurried back and pushed me away. "Are you okay?" he asked as the girl coughed.

"She knew the whole time! She could've warned our parents but she let them die." I covered my face and headed out of the cave. "She let them die."

Eli handed the girl her water pouch.

"I don't deserve your kindness," the girl said. "It's true. I couldn't save your mom, but I saved you both. She would've preferred it that way. Who took care of you after your house burned down?"

I remembered when Eli and I had run out into the field. We made it into the treehouse as we watched our house collapse into flames.

"Come with me," a farmer had said from the porch. He helped us down and took us into his home. He nursed our wounds and took care of us for weeks as news of our inheritance and our family's company were taken by the Kan. I plotted my revenge for days until one day, the farmer removed a wooden floor board and uncovered a box.

"Take this," he had said.

I peered in to see bundles of money hidden inside.

"You can use it to go anywhere, lead a new life as new people," he said. "Everyone thinks you're dead. You can be successful at anything you do and be whoever you need to be to survive."

My head throbbed as it all came back to me.

"She left you that money, Celio," the girl said with glimmering eyes. She rubbed them with her sleeve and put her contacts back in. "I tried to warn your mom, but she wouldn't listen. She knew the Kan would stop looking for her if they thought you and your family were dead. She wanted you to have a good life."

Tears burst forth, spilling down my face. My chin

trembled like a small child and I looked towards the light in the sky as if it could soothe me. I heard myself screaming from the inside, and it took everything out of me. My trembling hands punched at the ground. I couldn't stop. Everything was trembling, even the ground. Eli held me in silence. My tears soaked her chest as I clutched onto her jacket. I was the one Eli always cried on, why was it different now?

Once I calmed down, I wiped my eyes and turned my back on everyone as I stared at the forest. A cool breeze blew from the mountains, carrying leaves with it. I watched them fall into the maze below. "We can't let them get away with it," I said after a long silence. "We need to go after every single one of them. They don't deserve to live, not after what they did."

"Revenge will not solve anything," the girl warned. "If you're going to take them down, we'll have to do it the right way."

"We?" I yelled at the girl. "There's no we. There never was and never will be. You've done enough." I grabbed my bag.

"Where are you going?" the girl yelled after me.

"Far away from you!"

"That's a bad idea." The girl stood in my way. "Your mother died to protect you; you can't let her death be for nothing. Don't ruin your future going after the same people your mother has been trying to protect you from. Let me help you."

I slapped the girl's hands away.

"Come on, Eli. Let's get out of here." I reached for her hand and she snatched it away.

"No." Eli shook her head. "She's right. We need to stay here. She can help us."

"Did you not here a single word she said?!" My mind began to shut down, unable to think anymore. I barged out of the cave and froze at the edge. I could still see the forest around me, like a nightmare I couldn't wake up from, like the world that I knew was so far away. I picked up the rope from the ridge and looked back at Enura. "Take me down…now!"

Enura looked at the girl and she nodded. She rested her hands on Eli's shoulder and watched Enura lower me down over the ridge. Anger and bitterness left me as I tipped my chin up, hoping Eli would change her mind. The last thing I saw were

Eli's eyes piercing into mine, fixed and unchanging. My heart froze and my legs almost failed to hold me against the wall.

Goodbye, Eli.

CHAPTER SEVEN

Nick

SHLICK. SHLACK. SHLICK. SHLACK. The sound of metal scraping against metal woke me up. The soldier grasped a stainless steel whisk between his hands, as he turned it in the sieve. Back and forth the green weeds scraped against the ends of the sieve.

"Oww." I straightened my back and looked down at my leg, which had been wrapped in bandages. "How long was I out for?"

Sweat drenched the forager's clothes. He rolled up the sleeves of his jacket and wore a white flannel shirt underneath. Water boiled in a pot situated over a small hearth. It looked like a small glint of fire from a candle or stick that touched the bottom of the pot.

The forager scooped the dull brownish-green paste the weeds had formed and pushed them through the sieve to break up the clumps. He picked up a wooden spatula near a tea caddy and forced the paste through the sieve followed by a smooth stone. It shook the sieve until the entire paste dropped into the tea caddy. He poured the water from the pot, whisked the mixture until there were no lumps left in the liquid, grabbed the bamboo scoop again and scratched at the leftover paste in the sieve. With another hand under the scoop, the forager approached me. I pulled back.

"Don't move!" He lifted off the white bandages from my leg and poured the liquid over the gash.

I grunted. "What is this stuff?!"

"Be quiet!" The forager pushed me back down. "You come into my temple, bleed all over the floor and expect me to nurse you?" He pulled on the bandages tightly. I winced. "It takes an hour to stone grind matcha leaves into powder." The forager wiped the sweat off his forehead with the back of his hand.

I found a gas lit lamp placed over the shelf among other red lit candles that lined the bottom of the walls. The green wallpaper revealed swirls of stems and leaves that reached the ceiling. A change of clothes piled up in the corner below the shelf. The garbage bags next to it reeked.

"You're not a soldier, are you?" I looked at the empty contents of the black military bag behind the table. Weapons lined up the matted floor.

"I could say that it's a pleasure to meet you, Nick, but it really isn't." The forager pinned the bandages tighter.

"Oww." I winced. He dropped my ID onto my lap. My bag lay open by my side. "Uh-thanks?"

"I want you out of here as soon as you drink this." The forager blew the fire out under the pot, poured some more water into the tea bowl and clasped it with tongs. He poured it into a white stone cup and handed it over to me.

It smelled like hay.

"It's mixed with the spring water of Wakitsubo Lake." The forager rubbed his white and grey beard.

The green liquid tasted bitter, but felt creamy and tender after a couple more sips.

"Good." The old man turned to put away his tools. I eyed the cooking fish skewered over the hearth in the corner. The smoke rose through a black pipe that lined the corner of the wall and pierced through the ceiling.

I pulled myself up on my right leg, slowly lifted my left leg into a straight position, lowered the folds of my khaki pants over it and lifted my jacket off the floor. Holes from the fishing hook punctured my jacket's right shoulder where my badge number used to be.

That darn boy, so scrawny but so clever like this old man.

I felt for the belt, but found its pockets empty.

"Where are my things?" I asked as he lifted a fish from the fire. He skewered it to form a wave, as if the fish swam upriver, and roasted it over the charcoal. My stomach grumbled.

"Do you like sweetfish?" The old man turned his head back to me.

"This is really good," I told him, and spent the next few minutes gnawing on the third fish over a piece of bread on the center table. The old man wrapped the fish with lemon, cucumbers and mint.

"Ayu fish is the best in Aomori." The old man plucked the bones out of a fish in his hands. "The farmers call it Ayu, as in one year. We catch them days before they die."

"So you're a fisherman and a farmer?" I squeezed a lemon over the white flesh. "I haven't had a cooked meal in a while. So much for trying to find a new job."

"You?" The old man began to laugh.

"It's really not that funny. I invested my entire life into a, let's just say, a research that went wrong. I'm practically unemployed."

"With those tools I found on you, I thought you were a plumber." The old man continued to laugh.

"Well it's much better than being a farmer."

"No, no. I'm not a farmer." The old man waved his hand away. "I'm more of a garbage collector."

I rested my arms back and pulled myself away from the table slowly. "That darn lake," I hissed from the throbbing pain in my leg.

"I thought a black bear clawed you," the old man laughed. "Those lakes are dangerous. You'd be wise to stay away from the water."

"Well, it's a good thing I didn't break my neck tumbling down the slope on my way here. I'm lucky to have fallen into this … what did you say it was?

A Zen temple?"

"It's the temple of the white kami—it's better if you don't ask questions. I'm not supposed to help any contestants."

"Well, does a Zen temple have a bathroom?" I balanced myself on both feet.

"Down the hall."

I slid the wooden door open, limped into the dark, flicked one of the matches from my pocket and held it up in the air. A painting of a bald man with a grey moustache and beard stared down at me. He wore a navy blue robe and held a katana with both hands, ready to strike.

The next several portraits showed unknown faces of more men in robes until I reached the end of the hallway where a large family portrait hung from the wall. The bald man with the katana now sat in a wheel chair surrounded by five other members of what looked to be his family. A younger man with long grey hair stood on the left side of the chair and shook the hand of another man, bald, who stood on his right. They had the same eye color and body build—very much like brothers.

Woman dressed in red and yellow Japanese

robes held on to their man's arm. Six children crouched down in front of them, but none looked straight ahead like the rest. They seemed to have been nudging each other and fighting over their spots.

There was but one boy whose eyes caught mine in the portrait. He had a few strands of silver hair. I brought the match closer to his face and his red eyes brightened. He didn't smile and he had dull features about him, but his eyes carried a sense of danger, as though he was waiting for someone. Strangely, the soldier, the forager, the farmer, and the garbage collector, who all seemed to describe this old man that lived in this temple, were not in any of the portraits.

Who is he?

I lit another match to take a better look at the boy, and found another portrait next to the family one. The boy with the red eyes stood next to a taller man. He wore the same expression, while the man behind him rested a hand over his shoulder. When I crept closer I realized the man was much younger, like an older brother. I brought the match closer to the mole he had over his lip.

VHOOM.

The wall vibrated and made the sound of a vacuum.

VHOOM.

It came from behind a door. I slid it open, found boxes and bags piled on top of each other and walked through the narrow zigzag path between the mountains of garbage until I reached a corner where a small red flame beamed on and off.

Charcoal flooded the ground and felt warm, as they wobbled under my feet, reminding me of the pain in my leg. I grabbed onto the wall of boxes and bent down to take a look at where the charcoal led. They piled up under a hole in the corner and, when the flame beamed, a wide gush of smoke rose up the pipe hole, creating an explosion of dust and debris that clouded my face. I backed away, coughing and wheezing, and tripped over something on the floor.

I kicked away the charcoal, found a silver bracelet and pulled on it. The fallen charcoal exposed a dead hand underneath.

"Ahh!" I tossed the hand back into the char. Flies buzzed around in the dark and the smell of decay flooded through my nose when I touched the boxes.

Clothes, weapons, car keys, hair, shoes and bags and more bags of dead things covered the walls on my left, and papers and phones, and wires and rope and a muddy shovel covered the walls on my right, and badges and badges of all numbers lay by my feet mixed in with the char. Traces of things burned at the top of the mountain of charcoal. The smoke travelled up the pipe line.

I flicked on the last match and realized that I stood in front of a stovepipe hole. Trails of garbage led to the fire where everything in the room lined up to be burned. Some badges had letters on them; the white paint was peeled off, revealing a rusty metal underneath.

"A tracker?" I scrubbed the RF transmitter clean. The black paint of various badges protruding from a bag burned at the rim. Number six lay next to the bag. When I straightened up again I realized that it was actually a nine.

I picked up the badge.

6.

I turned it upside down.

9.

Which one was it?

"Seems like you found your way just fine." The old man's voice echoed behind me. I pushed the badge up my sleeve and turned.

"Ah, there it is." He lifted a root from a box. "Sweet Japanese ginseng."

"I should probably go."

"You were looking for your tools, weren't you?" The old man lifted a box and piled it on top of another to widen the path back to the door. "I cleaned them for you by the fire."

"Thanks." I walked through the door and paused. "You wouldn't happen to have any lithium batteries lying around, would you?"

The old man raised a finger in the air, then paced over to a shelf. "There." He put it in my hand. "Oh, I also left the money—"

"You can keep that." I felt the badge against my wrist. Losing a couple of bills didn't make a difference now. "You've got a weird family of pictures, eh?"

"They're not my family." The old man closed the door behind him. He lifted a jar off a shelf and opened it. Fireflies flew out, lighting up the hallway.

"I always go out at night and catch some before the next new hatchlings die. I spent my entire life on failed research too. See?" The old man raised the root in the air to point at the fireflies. "We're more alike than you think." The root touched his lips; he took a bite, hummed a tune in between murmurs and grabbed a cup of tea off the table when we walked through the sliding door again.

"I'm okay, thanks." I waved it away. I looked out the open door on the other side of the hall, where the sky changed to a light blue with the rays of the sun weakening. If it wasn't for the time, it would have looked like morning.

"I should get going."

"Stay out of that water, now."

"Will do." I stepped outside onto the wooden veranda and walked towards the red gate. The thin streaks of white in the sky and the color of the approaching sunset quivered in the reflection of the water. I realized that I didn't know how to get back to the base. I turned around to the temple again. When I touched the thin crack between the sliding door and the edge of the wall, I heard the old man talking on a black phone with a raised antenna.

"Hana," he said in Japanese.

I grabbed the lithium battery and slotted it into the camera. I held it up to record him.

"I miss you. How's Shouta? He must be eighteen now, eh? I look at the contestants' faces and wonder if I will ever see my son—if he will ever visit me in the forest…if he looks like me." The old man sighed and took another bite of his ginseng.

" …It's so lonely here," he continued. "Only the voices of the birds and the dancing Ayu fish keep me company, but after one year they'll be gone just like the contestants who come here and are never seen again. Even the fireflies die. I can't help but feel responsible for every one of their lives …The Mori are really going far this year. Pushing these kids to their limits and using them to fight their battles—"

The old man coughed. His chest heaved. All those years living in a temple with the fumes and the burning supplies, he must have bad lungs. I scanned the veranda outside where the other garbage bags lay and found scraps of paper that pieced together a map dated nineteen ninety-seven.

I looked back at the garbage bags where worn out shoes, torn clothes and other scraps and pieces of leftover human belongings remained. The old man spent more than a decade cleaning up the forest! I looked at him still talking on the phone.

"I don't know how much longer I have to be here for." The old man's back slouched against the table. "I'm growing old and I have a feeling the Mori will replace me with a younger man one day. I just hope to hear your voice—please, at least one phone call to hear y-your voice before something bad happens…to me…" the old man cried.

I let go of the door, tucked the map into my pocket, and turned away from the temple.

CHAPTER EIGHT

Fisher

MY FEET HIT THE BLACK GROUND hard, sending shockwaves to my brain. My legs were burning as they worked, propelling me forward at a sprint. My lungs heaved but the air just wouldn't go in. Rising panic and dizziness pushed me to fall but I had to keep running.

"You're not going to be able to run much longer," a voice laughed behind me.

I slammed my back against a tree and grabbed my trembling knees. Thoughts accelerated in my head. They wouldn't slow down. They wouldn't let me breathe. My heart hammered in my chest and the ground started to spin.

"Shall we kill him?" another voice echoed.

"S-stop..." I clasped my head.

"He's already dead," another said.

"Get out of my head!" I roared.

"Shall we kill him?"

"He's already dead."

"Enough!"

Silence filled the air as the murmuring thoughts came to a stop. I exhaled in relief.

"Maybe he is worthy, after all."

I froze. Three shadows encircled me, laughing, their faces blurring into one. One of them poked me in the chest. I spun around as another punched me in the stomach, grabbed my hand and whirled me to the side. I swung out with my fist, smashing it into someone's jaw. Two of them held my arms back. I kicked the third in the gut and pushed the others back as I ran. I tripped over twisting roots and went down on all fours. Laughter echoed all around me as I crawled back up. A shadow dislodged from a tree and tackled me. A fist edged closer to my face. Pain erupted from my jaw as a force of blood pooled in my mouth. My guts smashed together as all three rained blows on me. When I swung back at them, my arms went through their shadows and they disappeared.

"Who are you?!" I yelled.

"Who are you?" Three heads peered back at me from a tree, hardly discernible in the shadowy twilight of the forest. Their eyes swiveled wildly and their heads joined the trees again. I closed my eyes and took a deep breath.

"It's just a vibe," I mumbled. "I just need to wake up. This isn't real." But the pain in my stomach was real. I couldn't feel my face, either. I had never felt vibes become this physical before. I opened my eyes and everything was still. There were no more moving shadows. I exhaled in relief.

"There you are!" A boy slanted his face up at me.

"W-where did y—"

A number of arms rose from behind the boy and pushed me back. My feet ceased to travel backwards and the forest whirled around me like blur. Colors swirled as my head tilted toward the forest floor. The expected thump of the ground didn't come. I gasped and flailed my arms as I fell into an unending darkness...

***

Every muscle knotted up and I twitched awake. Sweat drenched my skin, my eyes throbbed, and screams vibrated in my ears. I gazed up at the hole above.

"Help!" I coughed dust. The darkness disoriented me as I crawled onto a wall. A paralyzing pain ran through my body, like ice. My teeth crunched over my lip and blood filled my mouth. "Help!"

"They can't hear you," a voice whispered.

My stomach contorted as I was smothered by an invisible hand.

"It's okay," the voice continued. "I'm just like you. We all are."

More hands touched my back. "How many of you are there?"

"Four … maybe five. That one over there doesn't say much. It's like he's not even there."

I squinted into the darkness, unable to make sense of a shape or figure. "How did you all get here?"

"They put me in here, just before you fell in," the voice continued. "I'm Sharon."

I shook the figure's hand. "Who are they?"

"Zzzzz," another voice hissed in the dark.

"There's always three of them," another voice quivered.

"We need to get out of here," I said, digging into my bag. I felt for my rod, but the wire was all tangled and the pole had snapped in several places. "Do you have your kits?"

"I have a torch," one said.

"Yeah, but with one battery," Sharon added. "I already tried."

I unwrapped a stick of gum from my kit and stretched out the aluminum wrapper. "Give me the battery," I said. I took the battery from a cold hand and slotted it into the torch. I rolled the wrapper to shape it like the battery and put it in on top. I clicked the switch and a small light sliced through the darkness, emanating from the torch's center. "There." I waved the torch around and met four faces marveling at me.

"It's so good to finally see," a girl with short hair said. "I don't even know how long it's been. I'm Maori."

"Yeah, you lose track of time when you're down here," a boy said. "You can call me Toshi."

"You all look so young," I peered down at them. They stood around me in a circle, their heads up to my chest. "Did they put you all down here?"

They nodded.

"Did they get into your head too?"

"I don't know how I got here," another girl said, wearing a jacket. "I can't remember anything."

"What's your name?" I asked.

"I think it's Yara," she paused. "Yeah, it's Yara." They all laughed.

"How can you all still laugh when we're trapped down here?"

"It's safer in here than up there," Maori said. She lifted her sleeve to reveal a gash that stretched from her elbow to her wrist.

"Oh my God." I knelt down to examine the wound. "You should treat that before it gets infected."

She shrugged. "I don't feel it."

The torch light landed on a kit with perfume and duct tape inside. I ripped the bottom part of my pants and rolled it around Maori's arm. Pieces of duct tape held it together.

"Thanks," she said.

The torch lit up the opening of the hole.

"Even with all of us standing on top of each other, there's still five meters to go." Sharon read my mind.

"Zzzzz," a voice hissed again.

I pointed the torch down the side of the wall to find a boy huddled with his knees to his face. He mumbled while he rocked back and forth.

"He's been like that for as long as I can remember," Sharon said. "Don't."

I walked over to him and placed a hand on his shoulder. The boy started screaming. A buzzing sound swirled around him. It stopped when I let go.

"I told you he doesn't say much."

When I stepped back, the boy stopped screaming. "Where does this lead?" I asked, shining the torch down the dim and narrow path.

"We didn't get that far," Sharon said. "We couldn't see anything until now."

"I feel sleepy," Toshi yawned.

"It's the air," I said. "There's not enough air down here. You have to stay awake. Come on." I broke the gum into five pieces and distributed them. I kept the last one for myself. "It's caffeinated." I took a sip of water from my bottle and offered some to the others, but they waved it away. Slinging things over my back, we headed down the narrow path. We walked for miles, the air thinning out the deeper we went.

"I'm scared." Yara tugged onto my arm.

"Before coming to this forest," I said, patting Yara's small head, "what did you do when you used to get scared?"

"My mom used to sing me a song."

"I told you that story," Toshi interrupted.

"No, you didn't," Yara argued. "My mom sang me a song when I couldn't go to sleep."

"No, my mom sang me a song when I couldn't go to sleep," Toshi argued.

"Okay, let's not waste our breath here," I advised.

"If your mom sang you a song, what was it, huh?" Toshi crossed his arms.

A wrinkle formed between Yara's eyebrows. "It was …it was…"

"Exactly."

"I hate you!" Yara pushed Toshi and ran down the path.

"Hey, wait," I called after her. "We have to stick together."

"We'll catch up to her," Maori said, dragging Toshi's arm with her.

"What about you, Sharon?" I asked.

"I used to get scared of bears," she said. "My father is a Kuma Hunter, though; he always kept me and mom safe—until a bear gashed his face."

"How do you know that?" My voice trembled. "I didn't tell you that."

"No, you didn't." Sharon paced ahead of me and disappeared down the path.

"Wait," I uttered. I caught up with them. We reached a soft mottled brown barrier that stretched from one caved-in wall to the other. Its center looked like an upside down turnip with a hole. I pinched a fluid that dripped from the interlocking chambers of the wall.

"It's like wax," I said. It glued my finger and thumb together as I struggled to pull them free. White eggs as big as my fist nestled into each chamber and the wall caved in and out, like it was breathing.

"What's in there?" Yara fingers pressed into the hole in the center.

"Don't!" I warned.

The wall shook as wax spilled out of all the chambers. The eggs hatched one by one as yellow and black striped creatures buzzed out of their chambers.

"Ahh!" Yara bellowed.

"Run!" Toshi's voice ricocheted off the walls.

The buzzing sound of the striped menaces thundered after us.

"Come on!" Sharon gripped my hand and pulled me in after her.

"What are they?" Maori yelled.

"Wasps!" Sharon screamed.

"Give me your bag!" I ordered Sharon.

"Why?"

My fingers slipped into her bag and pulled out four

brown paper bags. I blew air into each one and stuck a piece of duct tape around the opening. "Toshi, Yara, put these up on the walls."

"What?" Toshi yelled.

"Just do it!"

Sharon, Maori and I ran to the end of the path, with Yara and Toshi behind. A streak of moonlight came down from the hole above. I tapped the torch against the wall and the battery and aluminum foil fell out. "Give me your perfume!" I yelled at Sharon.

She emptied her bag onto the ground and picked up a spray can. I snatched it from her, sprayed her bag and lit it up from the fire that sparked when the aluminum touched the two ends of the battery.

"They're coming!" Toshi and Yara headed towards us.

I kicked the bag forward and, as the large swarm of striped creatures approached, I sprayed the perfume onto the blazing fire. It engulfed the wasps in a split second. They shrieked, curling in on themselves, suffering a seizure before dropping to the ground like ash.

"Ahh!" a voice screamed. Our heads jerked to the boy huddled against the wall.

"Oh, no!" I tried to rush towards him but Sharon jerked me back. We watched the rest of the wasps engulf the boy as he screamed.

"It's too late," Sharon cried.

The fire spread to the wooden pillars that held up the walls. Smoke rose out the hole as we breathed in the fumes. With each cough came a whistling sound. My chest wheezed and I collapsed against the wall. A long and white slender hand clasped onto my arm and my weary fingers clutched onto his wrist, propelling me upward. I stared into the eyes of a man, hanging from a dangling wire and peering down at me. His glasses and scarf shielded his face.

"The others," my voice cracked as I pointed through the blinding smoke. "Sharon!" I felt a cold hand on the ground by my side and pulled. A skinless arm dangled from my palm and I dropped it. Coal black sockets stared back at me. "No! Sharon!" I cried. "Th-the fire must've—"

Four other skeletons lay next to Sharon's, reflecting a yellowed white. Tool marks gauged into a bony arm of one, and a round hole marked the skull of another. A red jacket covered its back. "No ... Yara," I screamed. "I killed them!"

"No." The man grabbed my chin and jerked my head around. "The flames didn't touch them. They were dead a long time ago."

The man tightened a wire around me and I heard a click from around his waist. It pulled us up to the top. I crawled out of the hole coughing. Phlegm spilled out of my mouth.

The man twisted a bottle open and poured water over my face. "You've got the sight. It's what it does to you."

"I-I don't understand," my voice cracked. "I talked to them. I-I touched them. We even ate this-this gum!" I spat out a black ball of wax. "No—" I shook.

The man pulled down his scarf and his hair fell out of its bun.

"Y-you're …"

"Jun," he said. He grabbed my throat.

"W-what are you doing?"

"Calm down. I'm not going to kill you." He tilted my head to the side, and with tweezers in one hand, he pulled out a sting from my neck.

"Oww…" I massaged it.

"The Triplets." Jun hissed as he dropped the sting into a bag and tucked it into his kit. "I'm surprised you're still alive."

"What was that?"

"Venom. Did they say anything to you?" Jun snapped

his fingers at me. "Hey, stay with me …"

My back slid against the ground and water caressed my body. It bubbled around my outstretched fingers. Steam rose from its clear surface. It was impossible to gauge the depth, but the water was hotter the deeper it went. I was in the middle of a lake with a hole in its sea floor. Jun crouched near the edge, looking at me through his binoculars.

"Hey!" I waved my hands at him. "What'd you do to me? How do I get out of this..."

"Just swim!" Jun waved for me to come.

I swam over the hole in the ground, the steam licking against my skin. It died down once I reached cold water. I raised my hand in the air and Jun grabbed it, pulling me up. Water evaporated from my body. I felt rubbery and I itched everywhere. I realized I was naked. "Where are my clothes?"

"Relax." He pointed to my bag on the sand. "I'm not going to take your badge. It's not me who's after it."

"Who is?" I dressed myself.

"The Kan," a voice laughed.

A pang of horror hit me. "No." I grabbed my things to run.

"Stay here," Jun said, "and don't move. That's how

they get to you."

"He's one of us," two others joined in. The words sounded strangely in sync, bitter and venomous.

"You can't have him," Jun iterated. "Not even for a minute."

The bushes rustled as a shadow slipped from tree to tree.

"Any minute now." Jun looked into the trees and sighed. "Do I really have to spell it out for you, Masaki?"

A boy with a magenta Mohawk soared out of the trees. He did a back flip and landed in front of us. Blades on a chain spun in each hand. "Who's this guy?" He glared at me.

"I'm—"

"You see them?" Jun tugged on a rifle from his bag.

"Yeah, I see them," Masaki said, his pupils dilated. His body twitched and he flung his blade into the bark of a tree ahead. A red band hung from its point. A shadow came alive next to the tree and a boy, nursing his wrist, stiffly gazed back at us. "There you are!"

The boy ran as two others merged with him. Masaki dashed after them.

"That's your cue." Jun hurried me. "Go."

CHAPTER NINE

Maya

"Stay here," I told Eli, snuggling under her blanket and warming herself by the fire.

"Is he going to be okay?" she asked.

"He'll be fine. We'll go look for him after I get back." I slapped the dust off my arms and strapped the kunai to my waist. "Enura will stay with you."

"I didn't volunteer for babysitting," he whispered into my ear.

"Relax. It'll be just like babysitting Minoru."

"That's even worse."

"They're expecting me," I said. "I have to go lay out the plans to them before we make a move. It's almost sunrise." I pointed to the dark bluish sky outside the cave. I bent down on one knee and brushed a hair behind Eli's ear. "There's only twelve hours left, little one. It'll all be over soon."

I tugged on a torch from Enura's things and headed into the dark worm-holed end of the cave. White flickering lights from stones lit up the cave walls, revealing a twisted path that slid down a steep slope and down to a smooth curve. The walls arched a hundred feet above. I ducked behind the stalactites as bats flew past. Stalagmites dripped water from the arched roof, and more lights flickered from a crack in the walls that met ahead. I hunched over, dodging a few low roofed rocks and crawled through the crack. Two narrower paths with large openings awaited me on the other side. I avoided the steep one and got down on my knees to crawl through the other one. The cave became alive with hundreds of voices. My hands slipped over the wet floor and I followed the orange flicker against the wall. The narrow path opened onto a ridge that looked over a large body of water. Sharp stalagmites jutted out of its surface. I shivered in the cold breeze as I walked down the ridge and came to its end. The path continued two meters away, where loose rocks had broken up the bridge that connected them. I took a few short breaths, ran and rolled onto the edge on the other side. I walked for another mile, the voices growing louder, and reached a door. I cleared my throat, adjusted my jacket, and knocked.

The iron door squealed open.

"Irashai masen." A maid with an apron around her waist welcomed me from the door. She held a scanner in her hand.

I pinched one contact out, and stared into the scanner. It beeped red.

"Try again," I insisted.

The maid brought the scanner to my eye and it beeped red again. My fingers dug into the girl's ear, drew out an earpiece and brought it close to my lips. "It's me, Maya."

The maid remained still, smiling. I shoved the device back into her ear. She listened to the voice from her com and nodded. "Welcome, Maya Mori. A bath has been drawn and the change rooms are over there."

"Oh, so now they give me the Mori name. How sweet of them. Did they give you one too, I wonder?"

"The bath is over there." The maid continued to

smile.

"How do you do that?" I strode into the baths, removed my clothes and stepped into the warm water. After a while, I went inside one of the stalls behind and dressed in a pink and white kimono. "You can be so much more than just a servant," I said from behind the curtain, tightening a red band around my waist. "I don't understand how the Mori can just pass their name onto their recruits and then treat them like slaves."

The maid's palm brushed through the curtain. I handed her my string of blades. She still waited. I groaned and handed her my last blade. Straightening my collar, I slipped into Geta. I hated those wooden clogs. The maid held a spray bottle in her hand.

"Keep that away from me," I said.

She paused and then proceeded to spray me with perfume from head to toe. I headed past the stalls to the end of the corridor, sneezed, tilted my head to the camera in the corner, and a buzzing door opened. Music filled the air as I walked into a grand hall. A symphony played from above the central stairs. It rushed in and around the servants scrubbing and cleaning every inch of the place. I passed by men and women all alike with blank and empty stares. When I looked at them, they smiled at me without meaning. I steered away from the cleaning team and bumped into a tall figure. This one didn't smile. A streak of burns snaked down the side of his face. It struck through a tattooed leg of a spider visible beneath his hair line.

"You!" I gasped, remembering how I had fought him in the fire. "Y-you're alive?"

"As are you." A voice came from the staircase.

My eyes left the man in front of me and lingered to the top of the steps. Mr. Mori, with a long greying ponytail and dressed in a kimono, stood in the center. He clutched a katana in his hand. Its sheath touched the ground where his feet met. "Care to go for another round?"

***

In an old board room with a vaulted ceiling, I clutched the black-leathered hilt of a katana with both hands. Mr. Mori, slashing the katana delicately at the air and the lights of the ceiling dancing on his cool steel, dashed toward me. I held my blade evenly, leveled with my nose, and stalled his strike. I whipped around to clash his steel. It shivered under his compelling strength. A wretched grin split his lips as he throatily crooned, pressing closer to my face. With one knee down, my foot pressed firmly against the tatami mats, I used all my weight to thwart him. Dodging his arcing blade, I watched him bring it over his head, humming a low, swift tune when he swung it down. It split the mats in half just as I whirled around him and pointed my sword at his back.

"Very good." He beamed. "The Kan have taught you well."

"As have you," I replied.

Mr. Mori sheathed his blade and called for one of the servants watching from the door. "Bring in the tea," he said. Paper-thin doors slid to one side of the dōjō and maids ushered us inside. They set up the table and the tea set. A servant pressed a button on a wall and a metallic screen rolled up, revealing a tilted window with sunlight dashing in. I could see down the side of the Mountain with the forest and the maze below.

"How is my son?" he asked, sitting cross-legged on the floor and sipping his tea.

"He hasn't checked in with us yet," I replied, my gaze never leaving the view.

Mr. Mori cleared his throat as he waited for me to have a seat.

"Forgive me, but I must refuse. The Kan never allowed it, and I never had a taste for tea anyway."

"You see, that's what I like about you," he laughed. "Very direct and straight to the point. Very well, then." He waved the tea away and the servants along with it.

"We're setting up a trap tonight," I said, rolling out a scroll from my sleeve and placing it on the table.

Mr. Mori examined it and nodded.

"We'll need to use the taihō if this is going to work."

"How many?" he asked, breathing heavily.

"All of them."

***

A serious man with every muscle on his torso as

defined as an Olympic gymnast stood next to me in the elevator. He pressed his thumb onto a scanner and pushed level zero—the basement. The doors closed and we went down from level twenty. He folded his hands below his waist and his biceps, the size of my head, had a spider tattoo. He caught me looking at it and I averted my eyes. The elevator doors opened and blue beams flicked on one by one, lining the edges of the tunnel we stepped out into. The man waited in front of the elevator as I continued down the tunnel. Cries for help and the rattling of chains echoed from one tunnel. Whips, blades, chains, and other tools for torture hung from its concrete walls. I breathed in sharply as I passed it. I headed down another tunnel and a steel vault with blast-resistant airlocks came into view. I had been here once before and it didn't go so well…

It all started seven years ago, when I was in a glass-walled hotel suite, looking over New York's City lights. I was sitting on a sofa watching three teenagers play cards on the center table. They each had a matching red band around their wrists. One kept track of the score, tapping into his tablet. They called him Saisho. A man with long hair and a bear tooth chained to his necklace sat in an armchair with his eyes closed. Thundering blows shook the locked door of the bedroom. Whoever was in there, had been at it for hours. The front door clicked open and a guard walked in.

"She wants to see you," the armed guard ordered. The three teenagers scrambled to their feet. "Not you," the guard grumbled. "You." He waved me over.

The long-haired man in the armchair opened his eyes and watched me in silence. I stepped out through the door and, as soon as it shut behind me, a number of guards shackled my wrists behind my back. I grunted as they threw a black bag over my head.

"Where are we going?" My heart raced.

"Don't ask questions. The less you talk the longer you live," the guard growled. They escorted me down a staircase and into a car. We drove in silence for almost twenty minutes, taking several turns and then coming to a stop. The car door opened and arms hauled me out again. "Let's go." The guard shoved me through a door that buzzed open, and he dragged me up another flight of stairs. "Hurry it up."

"You know, it's hard to watch where I'm going, and this bag makes it almost impossible to breathe."

Arms hugged my legs and lifted me up.

"Hey, put me down." I bounced off a guard's shoulder as we went up the next flight of steps. Just as I was about to break myself loose, the guard dropped me onto a soft mattress and ripped the bag off my head.

"Now, now, that's no way to treat a guest." A woman with short brown hair grinned from her desk. She wore a red dress, and crossed her bare legs in her chair. "Un-cuff her."

The guard hesitated.

"Do I look like I'm joking?"

The guard searched for a key on him and the woman rolled her eyes. I sat up on the sofa, wriggled a pin in the lock and we all heard a click. I picked up the cuffs between my finger and thumb and held them in the air. "I don't suppose you want these back?"

"Leave us," the woman ordered.

"Yes, Kimura-san." The guard nodded and left.

I placed the cuffs on a coffee table and scanned the office around me. It was three times the size of the suite I had been holed up in for days.

"You must be … what do the American's call it … oh yes, jetlagged." The woman poured a glass of water and, with a tablet tucked under her arm, approached the sofa.

"Th-thank you." I extended a hand but she ignored me, crossing the room and taking a seat in a chair. She sipped from her glass.

"I don't think you understand how this is going to work," she said, putting the glass down on the table. My stomach ached and my throat was parched. "You give me what I ask, and I'll give you what you need. Simple." She tapped a finger against her tablet. "Maya Hara, seventeen years-old, charged with breaking and entering, possessing a weapon of mass destruction and … murder. It's a little too much, don't you think?"

I eyed the water on the table.

"Maya," she articulated. "That is your name, isn't it?"

The water bubbled in the glass and I closed my eyes. "Yes."

"I find it very odd that someone like you shows up at my door, equipped with everything for just the right situation and at just the right time. Interesting." The woman tapped her foot impatiently. She set her tablet down, checked her watch as she undid it, and sighed. She lunged out of her chair and dug her nails into my neck, hauling me off the sofa and pinning me against the wall.

"H-he …" Gasps of air escaped my mouth as my hands squeezed the woman's arm. She brought her cold eyes close and tilted her head from side to side.

"How many wish to be young again like you." She smelled my hair, breathing down my neck. "You have such good skin. It would be unfortunate for it to go to waste." She released her hold on me and I dropped to my knees, panting. "Now get up; we have work to do."

Mrs. Kimura's voice rang in my head. I could still remember it, even after seven years had passed. I winced from the memory and turned my attention to the steel vault that creaked from the howling wind in the tunnel. Massive metal bolts held by a combination lock extended from the door into the surrounding frame. I rotated the discs, listening to them click into place. The vault opened and a cold, tightly pressured air emanated from within. I knew the room like the back of my hand. Parts and pieces of warheads, missiles, explosives and hazardous ammunition lined the counters and shelves. I flicked a kit open to reveal a vial of red blood encased in a glass box with an electronic combination lock on it. It was propped on a book that had a spider symbol etched in its center. Sliding it slowly under the kit, my elbow knocked into a bar behind and the book slipped out of my hands. It landed on its edge and the spider symbol fell out. A USB was attached to its back. The rest of the book's pages were either burned, smudged or loose from the spine. I closed the book and propped the kit carefully back on it. A glass cabinet marked 'sensitive' caught my attention. I hid the USB in my sleeve pocket, and closed my hands around a metal case with USW written all over it. From the center of the room, a light shone on an empty pedestal, the same one that used to hold the venom seven years ago.

I remembered Jinan, Saisho's friend, surveying the tray of three glass vials on the pedestal. The hazard symbol was plastered around each one. "Is this it?" He asked. "We came all the way out here for this?"

"Don't touch it," I told him not looking away from Saisho's tablet. "Are you in yet?"

"They don't call me the first for nothing," he said, furiously tapping away on his keypad. An alarm sounded from the tunnel.

I breathed heavily and gave Saisho a piercing look.

"It wasn't me I swear," he said. "Someone must have manually set it off."

"The guards just exited the tunnel." Sannan popped in through the vault door. "They're leaving."

The walls budged and the vault door shook.

"Whoa, what was that?" Saisho held onto his tablet.

"Do you hear that?" I stepped out of the vault and pressed my ear against the tunnel floor. Water swooshed underneath. "Seal the vault."

"What?" Jinan's eyes widened.

"Are you crazy?" Sannan yelled. "We'll be locked in. We need to find a way out."

I sprinted to the vault door just as the wall of the tunnel collapsed and waves of water crashed through. I threw Sannan into the vault and sealed the door after us. The vault shook again and knocked out the shelves.

"What the hell?" Sannan jostled me.

"I just saved your life. The whole tunnel is flooded. Your friend here didn't trigger just any alarm. This tunnel is designed to flood in emergencies." I dragged a metal cased box and stood on it to feel the stone ceiling. "We're going to have to blow ourselves out of here." I rummaged through canisters on a shelf and drew out soft and moldable clay. "Help me get it around in a circle."

Jinan climbed on Sannan's shoulders as he plastered the clay onto the corner of the ceiling.

"How much longer till the tunnel is drained?" I asked Saisho.

"Two minutes," he said, tapping on his keypad.

"A little help here." Sannan wobbled as more shelves tumbled. Saisho let go of his keypad and squeezed Sannan's shoulders.

I stuck two cap fuses into the clay, pulling the wire back. Jinan jumped off Sannan and they took shelter. "You might want to cover your ears." I plugged the wire into the detonator. It sent a shockwave into the clay and it exploded, caving in the wall and sending rocks tumbling down around us. "Is everyone okay?" I coughed. A cloud of dust and debris filled the air. I kicked a shelf off me and searched the ground for the boys.

"Over here." A hand protruded from a tilted shelf. I clasped my fingers around it and dragged Saisho out. He secured two yellow vials against his chest. The third broken, leaving a yellow stain on his clothes.

"I tried my best," he said, coughing. "Do you think the Kan will be impressed?"

"Saisho." I slapped his face. "Stay with me." I pulled his arm over my shoulder, his forehead burning up.

"Where's Jinan and Sannan?" he mumbled. We spun around and searched the ground. Rocks piled on top of shelves.

"Sagasu …" Voices rang in the tunnel.

"There's no time." I pushed Saisho up to the floor above us, and climbed up after him.

"No, we have to come back for them." Saisho fought my grasps.

I sent a blow to his face and he slumped onto my shoulder. "I'm sorry."

Even after seven years, the vault was still the same size. I looked at the corner of the ceiling where Saisho and I had escaped. It was now replaced with metal. I headed back out into the tunnel, sealing the vault behind me, and hoping it would be the last time I'd have to come here.

CHAPTER TEN

Makoto

"WHERE IS MINORU?!" THE BALD MAN YELLED as he trudged in his wheel chair. The bald man's glass of water fell on the pink carpet.

"You have to take your medicine." Nurse Yu picked up the bottle of pills off the table.

"I'm not taking anything until I know how my grandson is doing." The bald man shook in his wheel chair.

"This won't do, Nurse Yu," I finally spoke from my chair at the other end of the dining table. I gestured for her to come.

"Yes, Mrs. Mori?"

I pulled myself up from the arms of the chair, felt for Nurse Yu's bowed head with my hand and slapped her.

"I'm very sorry, Mrs. Mori," Nurse Yu said.

"Hachiro!" I yelled. The guard at the door burst into the dining room. "See to it that Nurse Yu stays in her room until she is called for."

The door slammed shut and the nurse's struggles echoed in the hall. I reached into my robe pocket for the whip.

"You will not force me!" the bald man roared as he turned the wheels back.

I clasped the end of the table, held on firmly and walked over to him.

SNAP!

The whip smacked against the steel wheel. The bald man rolled forward.

SNAP!

I clasped the end of the whip with my other hand and wrapped it around the bald man's head. "Listen to me, Oji-san." I tightened my grip on the whip behind the bald man's neck, slapped my hand on the bottle of pills at the table, emptied it in his mouth, squeezed his lips shut, released the whip and waited for him to swallow. His breath came out in interrupted gasps. Drool spilled onto my hand.

"Good." I smirked, wiping my hand on his chest. "Don't sleep for long. In the next few hours, you're going to wake up and see that it's all over." I patted his bald ḥead. "Everything is going to be mine. Minoru is my son." I slipped the whip back into my pocket and took hold of the wheelchair, pushing it through the room. The doors opened and the guards stepped back.

A grandfather clock ticked in the distance. It came from Oji-san's room. Minoru's grandfather obsessed over time. He didn't spend a minute without making sure he knew where everyone was. He didn't want to die alone. He didn't want to include me in his will. He didn't want me to attend Minoru's birthday. He only spoke nicely to Minoru and I didn't know he was obsessed until I heard him and his lawyer exchange details of his will.

Minoru is going to take everything. I know it.

Oji-san snored in his chair as I brought him to the door. I searched for the keys in his breast pocket and fiddled with the chain until I found the right key. I unlocked the door and wheeled him inside.

"How much longer do I have to suffer?" I asked him, pulling his shoes off and throwing his legs over the bed. "I've almost gone through a bottle in one day. Putting them in your food, in your tea, and now you don't even eat anymore." I slid my fingers under his shoulders and, after several pulls, I managed to haul him out of the chair and rolled him onto the covers.

"Maybe it's better for you this way," I told the sleeping old man. "To die sooner. Then, I can get my hands on your will. I built this family. The game runs every year and ends on Minoru's birthday. Now that he is turning eighteen, it's time for him to become an adult, to lead The Mori Group."

The grandfather clock ticked, ticked, ticked...

"I took your son for a husband—a man who I thought could make his own decisions. Yet he follows you like a lost child. Nobody makes any decisions around here. The family would fall apart if it weren't for me. I deserve the inheritance more than anyone, don't you think?"

Oji-san snored. I fluffed up the pillows behind his head, reached for one more beside him, held it a few inches above his face and paused. A ticking sound against glass echoed near the bed. I put the pillow behind Oji-san's head and grasped the container near the bed where the black widow spider tapped its legs against the glass wall. It always sensed the gift I brought her each visit. "Shhh… now, little one." I rubbed my finger against the glass container and pictured a red hourglass on the spider's abdomen. Time was ticking away just as this little one ticked her legs against the glass. She needed to get stronger to protect her children. Soon she would starve, and when she starved she became agitated. That was the only time she ever bit anyone. I unfolded a plastic bag from my pocket, holding a smaller male spider—her meal. I carried him near the container. "Soon, my little one." I laughed at the poor creature. I was just like her, a starving mother, always wanting more power to protect my children—to protect Minoru, who needed me to be strong for him. And just like this mother, we were treated like Oji-san's pet, trapping us in a cage. A knock on the door startled me and I dropped the lid of the spider's container.

"No!" I bent down to feel for the lid.

"Honey, is that you?" A rough voice called out to me and the door swung open.

I hid the bag in my pocket.

"Is he okay?"

"Takeshi…" I straightened my back quickly and

bumped into the wheelchair.

"Easy…" Takeshi pulled me towards him by the shoulders. "Oto-san is getting old."

I took deep breaths before forcing a smile. "He thinks too much…Walk me to my wing, will you?" I raised my arm for Takeshi to hold.

"It's all because of the fire that this happened to you," Takeshi apologized for the hundredth time. "The summer heat in Italy had been too much. My men didn't think the fire would spread that far."

"It got our closest allies killed!"

"Hush…" Takeshi closed the door and led me down the hall. "The walls echo. Besides, we can always make new allies."

"Like that snake?" I snorted. "I heard you talking to her this morning. She looks different every day. Has she been tucking her tail between her legs after saving her from that fire?"

"She's gathered a trap at the base."

"I don't believe her story about the Kan just leaving her. That girl changes colors just like a snake. Once a snake, always a snake. She's a poison to this family."

Takeshi kissed my forehead over the bandages.

"It's going to be wonderful. I wish you could see it."

"I will." I clutched the whip in my pocket. Takeshi unlocked the door to my quarters and guided my hand to the frame of a settee. "I can take it from here." I turned around.

"Let me just open the door for some fresh air." Takeshi pushed the sliding doors from each other as the breeze blew the drapes away. "It's nice while it's still warm."

Takeshi squeezed his hand over mine.

"I have to get ready."

He pulled me closer to him.

"Takeshi."

He sighed and rested his hand over my shoulder. "I just want you to be happy."

"I still have a lot of footage to go through. I need to go see how my son's doing."

"Our son." Takeshi stepped back. "Why is it so hard for you to understand that I did everything I could to save everyone from that fire? In fact, you've been blaming me since the day I came clean to you about my other children. How long do I have to keep apologizing?"

"I'll see you at the base."

Takeshi walked out the door and I closed it after him. His training shoes echoed along the floorboards. They were the same black cotton sole canvas slippers that I used to clean for him. I had practiced martial arts in the dōjō with him for years...

"I love this dōjō," I told him many years ago. "We should call it the Golden Pavilion."

Takeshi laughed, squeezing my hand as we lay on the tatami mats, exhausted after a night's fight.

"Come on." I stared at the ceiling. "This is where Zen Buddhists practiced their meditation, the place of enlightenment."

These were good times, I recalled. But, not anymore. I sat in a chair by the dresser, took the hairpins off the back of my head, reached for the fold of the cloth and un-wrapped it from around my eyes. Crisped lines stretched over my eyelids, no longer bleeding. I stared into the mirror, but I knew that I would no longer look the way I was before. Not even tears could flow down my burned skin. Nothing could soften the scars on my face, not even the smooth and grounded matcha powder. I reached for the jar anyway and dipped my fingers into the cool cream. It smelled like green tea just as I had loved it. The film over my eyes felt hard. I would never know if my eyelids were open or closed. I couldn't feel anything there anymore.

I walked toward the breeze and felt the warmth of the sun. The sound of water from the bamboo trickling into the pond at my stone garden made me happy. Without Minoru, I only had one thing that could comfort me. I slipped my feet out of my slippers. The grass tickled my toes. I walked over the small rocks and gravel that lined the pond and wondered how my carps were doing.

"Koi." I called out their names and dipped my toe into the water. The fish nibbled at my skin. I crossed a small wooden bridge that arched over the pond to the island. It looked like a Horai, the Tao path that our people worshipped long ago. I felt the etched Japanese characters on a stone.

"For longevity and health." I pressed my hands together and bowed my head to the Tao. Straw, burlap and ropes were stacked on the right. Maids used them to insulate and protect my trees in the winter. Nets overtopped the shrubs to prevent the Mantema flowers from being damaged by insects.

Every year, I would find Mantema flowers diluted into a perfume laying on a stone. I touched the cold stone of the snow lantern in the center of the island, water flowing from the basins around it.

"Tsukubai," the forager had called them. "For ritual cleansing."

Water trickled down the bamboo dipper and into the basin. I grabbed it and scooped up the water to sip.

"Makoto?" a voice whispered from behind the fence that barricaded my garden. "Makoto …"

"Yes, I'm here." I recognized his voice.

"I made some more matcha—"

"Leave it under the fence."

"My family—"

"I need you to plant evidence that will lead back to that snake who thinks she's one of us now."

"Evidence for what?"

"For the death of Oji-san, head of The Mori Group." As soon as the words left my lips, I could hear the forager gasp. "Evidence in exchange for information about your family."

"But— But why now? After all those years I've known you…you would never—"

"You don't know me, Haruki."

"Y-you're right. I never really understood you even after all those years we worked together to build this…this contest."

"And you were the one who lost ten years ago."

"I withdrew from it. I gave up everything for you so you could be with your family and I could be with mine."

"Well, if you had chosen differently we wouldn't be standing on opposite ends of the fence!" I took a deep breath and lowered my voice. "You want to discuss the past? Fine, but we're running out of time. I left the container of the black widow open near Oji-san's bed. One bite could be fatal, especially while he's sedated. His body won't be able to fight it and he'll likely die from a stroke. If not that, then organ failure or a heart attack. It can happen in just a few hours, so I need you to plant evidence on this girl. You know where his room is. This is your chance to go over the fence so you can be together with your family again."

"And you will give me information in exchange?" The tremor in the forager's voice betrayed hesitation. "How do I know that you will keep your word?"

"Your son is among the contestants … I will tell you the rest after."

Water trickled once more down the bamboo dipper and into the basin. After a long sigh, I heard a soft "okay" from the forager before the water masked the sound of his footsteps backing away. Past the snow lantern, I touched the leaves of all the trees that I had planted when I was little. Oak, Beech, Walnut, Hornbeam, Katsura, and Kaloponax. I didn't stop until the spruce tree pricked my finger.

"It's a gold spruce tree," I had told Minoru when he was just five. "It's the only one left in this world."

"How come its needles are half gold, half green?" Minoru asked, a silver hair strand blowing against his forehead. I brushed it away. His silver strands were like the gold needles, smooth and beautiful. Its green ones were sharp and dangerous.

"It's half-albino," I said.

"Like me?" Minoru beamed.

"In a way, yes." I laughed. "I planted this tree the day you were born." I grabbed Minoru's chin and caressed his head. "Whenever something or some-one bothers you, I want you to come here and look at this tree. I want you to remember how special you are and that there's no one else like you in this world. Just like how there are two sides to this tree, there are two sides to everyone, the good and the bad."

CHAPTER ELEVEN

Shoji

A WHITE CIRCULAR BUTTON beeped orange down the dark and quiet cave. Outside the cave's opening, the helicopter that dropped me off sped away and drowned the voices of contestants that dropped twenty stories below. Once the wind from the propellers of the helicopter calmed, a noctuid moth fluttered its black and yellow striped wings as it landed on the wall of the cave near the elevator. I withdrew a bundle of keys from my pocket and shook it. The wings of the moth twitched. The moth darted to the ground and remained still.

***

"Noctuid moths always confuse high frequency

sounds with echolocating bats," a man had said to me once. He carried a round metallic device, pushed a button in its center and the moths suffered a seizure, plummeting down to their deaths. "Sonic waves," he said. "Too bad they're deaf to all other sounds including humans.'"

I helped him dress into a white lab coat and covered his hands with latex gloves. He used a set of tongs to pick up a vial and I tightened the lid around it.

"Shoji, what are you doing here?" Akane, a young woman with short brown hair, peeped at us from the door.

"I like to help sometimes," I said.

"You're a business man, born to lead the Hideki Group, not a scientist."

Makoto barged in through the door carrying a centrifuge. "Is it ready yet, Haruki?"

"Almost," he said.

Makoto set up the centrifuge on the counter. "Kimura Akane," Makoto scolded. "Stop flirting with Shoji and get over here and help."

"Hai," Akane saluted and I laughed. "She's so bossy," Akane whispered. She then pressed her hands together and mouthed, "Help me."

Haruki placed the vial carefully into the centrifuge, and turned it on. We all watched for a few minutes.

"Is this really going to change the world?" I asked.

"If Haruki made it, then yes," Makoto said with a nod.

The centrifuge came to a stop and Haruki held up the vial with one gloved hand. We all bent down to examine the yellow fluid.

"Sorry I'm late!" A woman with chestnut hair ran into the lab. "It's really hard figuring out which train to take when everything is in Japanese."

"You came just in time." Akane hugged her.

"This is Amelia, the one I told you about," Haruki whispered into my ear.

"Nice to meet you." I shook her hand.

"Sucks that a bunch of us grad students have to spend a Saturday night in the IST lab," Amelia teased.

"You wouldn't want to miss this." Haruki showed her the vial.

"Good thing I brought my camera." Amelia held it up. "Smile."

***

I headed deeper into the cave, pushed a circular button and waited in front of an elevator. The orange light dimmed from the button and the elevator doors opened.

"Welcome to The Mori Group residence," the automated voice activation system chimed.

I inhaled, took one step inside, stared at another door opposite me and pushed level one.

"The Moris are believed to be the descendants of the royal samurai clan dating back to the twelfth century," the voice activation system continued. "They preserve one of the only forests in the world to inhabit more than five hundred new and endangered species of flora and fauna. The Moris occupied the forest for years, until they sold the lower half in the Akita prefecture to the Hideki Group. The Moris come from a long history of ancestors and Kuma Hunters—"

"Yeah, yeah..." I pushed the button several times, as though it would make the elevator go down faster.

"—and, ever since, they have been preserving the forest to protect its species and history from becoming extinct. I hope you enjoy the rest of your journey, and take care."

The elevator doors opened into a long, dimly lit corridor. I followed the torches along the walls of the cave and reached another metal door. I looked at the camera hanging from the corner.

"Hideki Shoji, irrashai masen," another voice activating system answered. A retinal scan situated near the gate flashed red. I leaned over and it scanned my eye. The door buzzed open.

I walked down another corridor until I came upon a red door. I grasped the iron handle, pulled it to the side and closed it after me.

"Welcome, welcome." Two maids in white approached, one holding a white towel, the other holding white slippers. "This way," one of them said, gesturing down the long white hallway. The white fluorescent lights reminded me of a hospital. "Your bath has been drawn. Please leave your clothes in this basket, and you may only wear the traditional kimono when greeting the Moris. Please leave any weapons behind—"

I shoved past the maids.

"Matte Kudasai!" One of the maids grabbed my arm and I slipped through her grasp. Two armed men approached.

"Are we seriously going to do this again?" I dropped my jacket, rolled up my sleeves and held my fists up. The maids unsheathed their blades. One spun the hilt of a kunai around her finger. The two men drew their katana and circled me. The tapping sound of a cane jerked us away.

"Children, children," Makoto interrupted. She looked beautiful in a dark blue kimono patterned with yellow and white Mantema flowers. A touch of red on her lips made me forget her accident. "Hideki-san is our valued guest. It's very poor judgment of you to consider him a threat."

The staff concealed their weapons and addressed their attire to look the part as they bowed to greet Mrs. Mori. I couldn't mistake any of her assassins for a regular employee.

"Come, Hideki-san. This way." Makoto turned her back and I followed her. We walked down a white corridor and, the further we went in, the walls transitioned into a traditional Japanese house. The yellow wallpaper of the sliding bamboo doors came into view. The bamboo floorboards creaked with every step and the smell of incense burned my lungs.

The corridor split into the west wing on the left and the east wing on the right.

"There are no cameras beyond this point," Makoto informed me.

I slid my hands around her waist and hugged her from behind so she wouldn't escape. Her neck smelled of Mantema flowers, her hair of matcha.

"We need to talk," she said, her voice firm as always.

I exhaled intensely and released my grasp. She walked me into a room at the opening of the west wing and lit a lantern inside. I slid the door shut behind me, felt for her sleeve, pulled her toward me, and grabbed her flinging wrist. She dropped her cane. I caught her other wrist, turned and held her firmly against the wall.

"Don't," she whispered, turning her head to the side.

"Oho, what happened to the fighter in you, Makoto?" I grinned. "Did a little fire get to you?"

She faced me, her eyes blinded by the bandages, and pulled on my collar. "You were late." She smashed her forehead into mine, swung around and knocked me off my feet. Before I knew it, I was lying on the floor with her legs around my waist. Her blade tickled my throat.

"I love it when you get angry."

"I really meant what I said."

"So you really did call me to talk—"

"I fought the Italians one by one in that fire. What took you so long?"

"I got held back by the Kan, but I'm here now, aren't I? If I hadn't told you about their plan to take you down with the rest of the Italians, you wouldn't be here either." I traced the shape of her eyes under the bandages and cupped her face.

"Don't." She tilted her head to the side.

"Oh, come on. It's hard pretending to be allies with that woman. I'm sorry I couldn't come help you in time. Maybe then the fire wouldn't have hurt you like this. Plus, I got some good information from Akane. They built something big after that fire two months ago."

"Let me guess, another one of their experiments?"

"They're calling it the seventy-seventh Emperor. You know the one who put an end to the assassins and established the royal samurai clan? I can't remember what they're calling him but all I know is that he's deadly." I pulled on the bandages around Makoto's eyes and heard a crash. I pulled myself up on my elbows. A scream followed.

"What was that?"

"That's Nurse Yu." Mrs. Mori released me and felt the floor.

"I don't suppose you will be needing this?" I handed her the cane. "You swept me off my feet pretty quickly."

She grinned, retracted her blade, sheathed it in the cane and walked out through the sliding door. We strode to the end of the west wing and followed a crowd of staff to the entrance of a bedroom.

"Oji-san!" Makoto ran from my side, through the crowd and to the old man in the bed. She felt for his pulse. I sighed and pushed through the little assassins.

"He's dead." I looked at his eyes. "I would say around an hour ago. He's still warm." I raised the bed sheet, found a long yellow strand of hair on the body, sniffed it, looked down and found two small puncture holes in the middle of a swollen white circle on the old man's chest. "A bite mark?"

"I-I found the container open, Mrs. Mori," Nurse Yu stuttered. "The sp-spider, its gone!"

Makoto slapped the nurse across the face. "What were you thinking?!" She kicked the nurse to the floor and raised her cane to beat her.

I grabbed the cane. "I think what the nurse here is trying to say, is that a little girly, possibly blonde, was here." I searched for the phone in my pocket and flipped it open.

"It was that Kan girl. I know it was her!" Makoto grabbed my arm. "If only Nurse Yu had arrived on time to wake Oji-san up, this wouldn't have happened."

Nurse Yu cried on her knees.

"I know a guy," I said. Everybody looked at me. I recognized many of them as contestants from the past decade.

"No, no cops," some whispered. They looked at me with wide eyes as though scared for their lives. I wondered how many crimes the Mori Clan would get accused of, how many of those children in front of me would spend the rest of their lives in jail. Makoto would find anyone to pin this on. I dialed the number on my phone. "We have a situation …"

"Where's my husband?" Makoto cried. Takeshi walked in the second after.

"Oto-san! Oto-san!" He ran to the bed and shook the body. "What happened?" He looked at Nurse Yu crying and his eyes followed the cane nearby till they landed on Makoto.

"I heard Nurse Yu scream and I came here as soon as I could—"

"Where were you?" Takeshi snapped.

"She was with me," I explained, covering the mouth piece on my phone.

"We were in the middle of a meeting—a shareholder's meeting," Makoto continued, "and Oji-san was lying so still." She shook her head. Makoto was never sad.

"I found this hair." I showed the strand to Takeshi. "I know a guy who's very discrete. He'll get it scanned at the police station just like that." I snapped my fingers. "He won't say a word."

"No, no. I don't want any police on my property,"

Takeshi said quickly. "I don't want them to poke their noses around here. This is private property." A sweat trickled down his forehead. Was he nervous?

"Moshi, moshi …" a voice answered the phone.

"Can I call you back?" I cupped my mouth. "Ok, ok." I hung up. "Do you have a DNA gel electrophoresis?"

"Hideki-san, Mori Group is a biotech company. You can find everything you need at our research facilities downstairs. I will take you." He raised the white sheet over the body, paused at the head, closed his eyes and released it. I followed him through the crowd and took one last look at Makoto sitting by the side of the old man's bed, resting her head on the cane.

"It just doesn't make sense," Takeshi said with an upturned mouth, a tense look in his cold eyes and a wrinkled forehead. "Everyone in this family was raised with Moris. We've all been bitten, we've all become immune, and even one bite wouldn't kill this fast. Something's wrong."

"Well there are two possibilities here. Either this Kan girl, Mak—the one Mori-san keeps talking about—injected your father with a higher dose and staged it to make it look like it was the spider, or..."

"Or what?" Mr. Mori walked me away from the door and gestured for me to keep going as we went down the west wing.

Or this whole crime was staged by your wife...

"Look, I'm no doctor here, but I know when there's been a struggle prior to death. I watch a lot of contestants die, Mori-san. I study them, examine every condition and trace every single injury back to its kill. If your father is as immune as you say so, there wouldn't be any swelling. But there was. It was cardiac inflammation."

"What does this mean?"

"Many autopsy results report cardiac inflammation in heart attack victims. I'm sorry, Mori-san, but I believe that based on my analysis of his condition—"

"You think he died from a heart attack?!"

"Yes."

Takeshi seemed impressed by my deduction.

"Does your father take sleeping drugs by any chance? One bite of a spider like this combined with the drug effect can induce a heart attack.

There are many forces at play here and I suppose the person this hair strand belongs to will have the answers."

Takeshi grabbed a receiver off a guard passing by.

"Send forensics from the lab to scan for any fin-gerprints," he ordered into the device and tucked it into the guard's trouser pocket. He turned around the end of the west wing and headed down the corridor that led to the elevator, giving orders to a few approaching men as they bowed and took their leave. A door from the east wing opened to a garden. A figure shifted among the bushes. More guards ran past me, followed by forensics in blue face masks, yellow gloves and white uniforms.

"Mind if I smoke outside?" I took out my pack. "I know where the lab is. Here, it'll only take a minute." I handed forensics the strand of hair. One of them locked it in a plastic bag. Takeshi continued down the dark and torch-lit corridor. I watched him till I could only see his mere shadow turn at the corner. I tapped the pack against the side of my leg. One cigarette popped out. I tucked it between my lips, headed to the open door and smelled Mantema flowers along with a mix of matcha.

"It's time to speak up," I heard a whisper. "Where's my son?"

The figure sat on a white stone, and I gradually recognized it as Makoto.

"Everything I do is for you. I want to go home, Makoto. I regret ever working in the labs, ever creating this game with you. T-this forest ... all it has ever done is cause harm to these contestants, we have been causing them harm. It's enough. No more games, Makoto."

I lit the Seven Stars cigarette.

"Your son is Minoru, Haruki," Makoto said. She took a sip of the basin water with the bamboo dipper, her shoulders lay calm, her stand lay firm and her face lay without expression.

I puffed.

"Is this a joke?"

"He's turning eighteen soon." The bamboo dipper dropped into the water basin. "It's been almost eighteen years, Haruki."

I puffed.

"All this time...All this time you have been lying to me." A shadow dispatched from underneath the golden spruce tree and joined Makoto's shadow. Long hair fell from his head, torn clothes from his body, and the stench of garbage hung in the air. "I only have one son, Makoto, and his name is Shouta. I have a wife waiting for me. I haven't seen her in ten years! My son was just a little boy when I left him. You lied to me! You said you'd give me information about my family, but you're not my family, Makoto."

"Your wife is dead," Makoto said. The shadow trembled and leaned against the fence.

"I dispatched one of my children to locate her in Aomori."

"How long have you known?"

"She died two weeks ago… I'm sorry."

"You're lying!" The shadow shook Makoto. "You're lying!"

"Shhh…keep your voice down."

"What about my son? My son Shouta." He shook her again. "Did you kill him too?"

I threw the cigarette and crushed it into the ground with my foot until all the tar squeezed out. I had been trying to quit but I didn't think I'd be able to now. Makoto shrugged her shoulders and shook her head. The man released his hold of her shoulders. "Villagers say he went searching for you."

The man pushed Makoto away.

"Haruki?" she called after him. He climbed up the tree and over the fence. "Haruki?"

"Hideki-san?" a voice behind me called. I turned around to see a young forensic girl speak from a white mask around her face. "Mori-san is waiting for you."

"I'll be right there."

CHAPTER TWELVE

Enura

"HOW MUCH LONGER?" ELI HUGGED her knees close to her face. She rocked back and forth with an empty cup of ramen by her feet. "I can't hold it in much longer."

"She'll be here soon," I assured her, putting out the fire.

"Why can't you take me? My brother always does it," Eli pouted. "I can just hide behind a bush. It won't take long."

"When Maya comes back, she will take you," I insisted.

"Take her to do what?" a voice echoed in the cave as Maya appeared.

"To pee," Eli and I answered at the same time.

Maya slowly put down a metal case of USW; her

blades clinked against each other at her side.

"A sonic weapon?" I turned my back to Eli and whispered to Maya, "Wouldn't that cause a blast?"

"Not if we set it up correctly," she explained.

"I really need to go," Eli complained.

Maya knelt down and opened the case. "It's got a variation of frequencies." She revealed a circular device. "Even the lowest frequency can make them go crazy. With the venom coursing through their veins, their senses will be enhanced enough to pick it up. The rest of us won't hear a thing."

"How do you know all this?" I asked.

"Think of it this way: When they come too close to the light, they'll drop like flies. They're not called the Kan for nothing, you know. K-a-n, the sight—"

"The Ki."

"Hello?" Eli urged. "Guys!"

"What?" We both jerked our heads around.

"Let's go!"

"Right." I rolled up my sleeves, flinching from the pain in my shoulder, and bent down to pick up the case.

"I've got it." Maya smiled.

We clambered down the ridge and back into the

maze. We followed the rocky path almost a mile before it went out into the forest. Eli skimpered to the nearest bush while Maya kept watch. I sat on a nearby rock sharpening my blades.

"I wonder where Celio is," Eli said from behind the bush. "We shouldn't have let him go by himself."

"He's a big boy now; he can take care of himself," Maya said, her arms crossed and her back toward Eli. "Besides, once the initial round is over, I'm putting you on a plane."

"With Celio?" Eli complained.

"With or without him. You and your brother made a big mistake coming here."

"If you've been looking out for us this whole time, where were you when I was kidnapped?"

"I was there the whole time. I wanted to see what your brother was like in the field, and I came to the conclusion that he's got what it takes to make it out of here. You don't. If he wants to be found, then so be it, but he shouldn't risk your life for his mistakes."

"I'm not going without him," Eli insisted. "If I go, he goes."

"We'll see about that. Are you done now?"

"Yup. Can I have a tissue?"

"Enura," Maya called as I set up another trap. "You got any tissues?"

"In the bag," I said, not moving. Maya marched to the fence, bent down to my bag, and picked up a packet of tissues. "I really hope this works," I said, eying the case.

"It will." Maya squeezed my hand. When she tried to let go, I squeezed back.

"Maya, you know I would do anything for you, right?"

I recalled the time when the alarms went off in The Mori Residence seven years ago. How the building had shook and the floor had collapsed under my feet. The pain of my head whacking the ground. The ringing in my ears. A good dozen men went down with me. I'd squinted through the smoke and dust to see Maya, just a girl, and a boy climb their way out of the vault...

"After them!" Guards ran down the other side of the corridor. The hole in the floor kept them at a distance as they tried to find a way to cross over. They aimed their guns through the smoke and debris. "Shoot at everything that moves," one of the guards had ordered.

A boulder trapped my leg as I tried to crawl free. My eyes found a blade in the distance and I stretched my fingers toward it. Maya and the boy limped past. She kicked the blade away, shots rang out, and they disappeared around the corner.

Blood spilled next to me from a man's arm as he groaned.

"We got five men down!" I shouted. In the thick cloud of dust, I reached my hand up towards the guards. "Don't shoot..."

The bulletfire stopped and I exhaled in relief.

"Keep shooting!" someone barked. "We can't let the intruders get away. It's their lives for ours. Get me security on the line. I need to see where this corridor leads."

Gunfire reverberated through the residence.

"No!" I yelled, ducking my head. Cold hands brushed under my arms and heaved. I turned around to see Maya. "Let me go," I grunted, squirming out of her grasp.

"I'm trying to save your life," she said.

I kicked the boulder with my other foot as she dragged me across the floor and to the corner. She dropped me down against the wall, the boy next to me on the verge of losing consciousness. I saw her whisk away a bundle of blades from the waist of a stiff body. Shots halted one by one. Turning my head down the corner, I saw Maya disarm all the guards. She ran back to my side, lifting the boy up by the arm.

"Why did you do that?" I asked, feeling faint from my bleeding leg.

"I don't want anyone dying because of me," she said.

"Enura?"

I jerked back into the present.

"Thank you," Maya said unsteadily as she drew her hand away and trudged back to the trees. "Here you go," she bent down behind the bush. "Oh, no."

"What?" I turned around, carrying the case.

"She's gone."

I rushed to Maya's side to find the bushes clear.

"We have to find her!" Maya panicked, her hands rubbing against her head. "We don't have time for this."

"Here." I handed her the case. "You go do your thing. I'll find her. She couldn't have gone far anyway."

"No, I should do it," she said. "I already failed them once. I can't do that again."

"Hey." I put the case down and rested my hands on her shoulder. "Everyone's lives are at stake here. Only you know how to set up these traps. I'll find her. She couldn't have gone far. Now, go."

CHAPTER THIRTEEN

Minoru

FOR THE PAST THREE MORNINGS, Shirakawa did a hundred and fifty push-ups, a hundred chin-ups from a tree branch, and amputated trees with a number of blows. Sometimes he stopped to do a plank for an hour, the bear tooth drooping from around his neck, but most of the time he walked. He never slept, and would sit cross-legged at night near the lake, his arms crossed, eyes closed, and his long black hair dangling down his back. He never ate and, if he did, I never saw him. He eyed moving objects and smelled them from a distance, but never approached them. Shirakawa lived a dull life. He could spend hours staring into the water, never drinking from it. For three days, my life had been all about Shirakawa. Shirakawa did this, Shirakawa did that. No weapons stood out on him, no badges, no food, money or any other kind of accessory. Shirakawa was just Shirakawa.

I watched the setting sun and its reflection in the lake. Ossan taught me this trick when it came to reading the time by examining the sun and its reflection in the water. The lake's circular shape and concaved edges reflected things around it at a certain angle. Ossan used this trick to locate objects or even people that fell in. It must have been almost eight o'clock at night. Soon, the moon would appear and darkness would mask everything around us.

I remembered when Mother would walk across the bridge trail over the lake at night. Mother loved to see it, but only at midnight did the black water lake shine.

Shirakawa took longer than usual this time, watching the water and waiting. I crawled slowly over the tree, the pointed blades from my soles pushing me up. I peered over the branch to look into the water. Shirakawa's reflection smiled at me. A poison needle swept past me and pierced the bark of the tree I crawled on. My ear almost touched it. I covered my nose and mouth and jumped from the branch, coming face to face with Shirakawa.

"That was very smart of you," Shirakawa grinned. "Had you moved any later, one sniff of that would've killed you. Omoishiroi ne?"

I drew all six kunai, each hand trembling for blood, and paced around my prey. Every time he had kneeled by the water, he waited. He waited for me to attack. That's what he watched for. I lunged at him from all directions. His black trousers tore above the knee and behind the calf. His sleeve tore from his shirt, and the kunai screeched against his shoulder blades, leaving three wide red marks in the center of his chest. I grabbed a tree branch and swung myself over it to watch my prey fall. Shirakawa stabbed me with his deep black eyes but held no expression. The wound on his arm from the torn sleeve closed and his chest healed. He didn't shed a drop of blood.

W-what? I leaned over the branch. *How...*

"Is that all?" Shirakawa cracked his neck from side to side, crossed his fingers and stretched his arms.

What are you? I tightened the black wire strings that held my kunai blades together. Each three circled around each other to form one pointed end. I wrapped the rest of the wire around my palms and gripped them tightly. Shirakawa reached for his legs and pulled an ice pick-shaped bone from inside his skin.

"Why don't you come down from that little tree you're hiding in?" Shirakawa sneered. "Unless you need a little help." He cocked his head up the tree as he approached.

I snared back, swung around the tree to the other branch and crawled my way up. I hooked the wire of my blades from a branch, plunged from the tree and aimed for Shirakawa's head. Shirakawa crossed his weapons over his face and dodged the kunai. I skidded around him and lunged at his back. He bent down, side-blocked my blow and tried to kick my legs from underneath me. I rolled away from him, hooked the other end of the wire on the branch of another tree and lunged back. Our weapons clanked back and forth and I jumped from tree to tree. I wrapped the wires around the bones and pulled each and every one of them out of his grasp. I finally had him surrounded by my web of wires, his two bones dangling from opposite ends of the web. I leaned against a tree to catch my breath.

"Still playing the game of hide and seek." Shirakawa tried to break through the wires that chained him in the center of four trees. He scraped his forefinger and thumb across the line to feel it and sucked on the blood that oozed there. I watched his wound heal again. Nobody told me about this. I remembered Masaki's scarred chest, barely escaping with his life, and how Maya had fought by his side when she was with the Kan. Did she lie to us? How could she fail to mention his ability to heal?

"Which one is you?" Shirakawa pulled on each wire around him. One squeezed tight around my waist. The sun had set, leaving faint streaks of orange and purple. Darkness loomed among the trees. A silent wind breezed through. I wiped the sweat off my forehead, my breath lodged in my throat. Only thirty minutes remained till the countdown was over and for the clock to sound the end of the initial round. A black narrow figure contorted on the ground. I grabbed its head. The tongue of a snake snapped back at me.

A mamushi?

I glanced at one of my kunai, then at the tongue

of the snake. I only had one move left to try and I needed more wire to do it. I loosened the kunai, dipped it into the snake's mouth, drew it out as the snake wriggled away, and pulled on one of the wires that locked Shirakawa's legs.

"Found you." Shirakawa grinned, wires snapping from around one hand. He eyes followed the end of the string that pulled on him.

I drew in a deep breath, forcing my hands to stop trembling, then I cut the wire loose from around my waist. His hands came free as I came out of my hiding.

"That's right." Shirakawa smirked, his legs still trapped. "Best to surrender now than later. You're awfully brave, well, for a little boy."

"I'm not a boy."

"Oho, so you do speak. I was beginning to think Japanese wasn't your language."

"Language is a mere string of words." Like those wires, I thought. They cut deep. "But I prefer to let my weapons do the talking." I hurled several of my kunai at him and watched him dance through the web, dodging every single one of them. He had twisted himself, getting the wires around his leg freed by my kunai. He had one leg left to free, and I had one poisoned kunai to save for last.

"Why don't you just give me your badge and I might just let you go?" Shirakawa expressed his agitation. It was so subtle that, if I hadn't been watching him carefully for the past few days, I wouldn't have cared. I thought this man to be expressionless, a predator with no emotion.

"I know you, Minoru."

I cringed. I can't let my guard down now. I searched for an opening.

"I know that you have never killed anyone before. Do you really think that you can kill me?"

I gritted my teeth. "Shut up!"

"See? That's the little boy I know. The one who can't live without his mother."

"Don't talk about Mother!" I hurled the kunai through the web toward Shirakawa. At that point, everything became clear. The whistle of the blade and the rising stench of blood all seemed to freeze. The scuff of movement, the hissing of a ragged breath, and a cry pulled me from my trance.

The Kunai had lodged itself into the throat of a little girl, who stumbled forward and then slumped to the ground. I watched blood pool around the girl's chestnut hair until Shirakawa met my eyes.

"You son of a–" I lurched on him and we rolled down the steep slope into the lake.

SPLASH.

I broke the surface of the water, climbing over the tipping point of the hill. I looked back at the blackwater, hoping to never see that monster's face again. Blood surged from the dying girl's lips, her life's blood continuing to drip from her heaving chest and splattering onto the ground. She looked at me with her blue eyes shocked into stillness.

"No!" I fell to my knees. I shook the girl's dead body. A black bird flew above. "Mother!" I bellowed after it. "Mother!"

CHAPTER FOURTEEN

Nikki

MANY CONTESTANTS BEGAN TO WANDER in toward the center of the base. I checked the ticking digital clock above the empty security office. Ten minutes left. My legs ached as I walked over to the center of the base.

"You're going to have to walk," the Director had said. "Just because Hideki-san pays us to do the spying, doesn't mean I have to drive you to the base. I'm keeping my RV far away this time."

I remembered how contestants had ransacked the RV at last year's contest, searching for food, or anything that could help them win.

Kuma Hunters waited around the base. Some of them stood in front of the empty security office, hands on their coms ready for further instructions. Two youngsters held onto each other as they walked, others dropped their bags and collapsed onto their knees. I heard sobs here and there. An American stood nearby with his arms crossed. His blue eyes glared at me. Leaves rustled in the trees that surrounded us. I slid a finger over a remote in my pocket and three black woodpeckers, like vultures, flew in a circle over the base. A fourth one landed on a tree behind me and another pecked on crumbs that a man with a bear skin had tossed. The man was laughing with a group of ten people around him. Aya Hideki leaned against a tree next to them, massaging her heel.

"She's late," she told her bodyguard. "She better get me back badge number seven from that scrawny little girl, or I'm gon' have to have a word with my father about this."

The sound of metal clinking on metal echoed from the trees and a figure sprinted out of the bushes, running towards me.

"We need to get everyone out of here," a boy said. I noticed a case strapped to his back.

"What's going on?" one of the contestants asked.

"Look here." I eyed the boy. "You need to take a step back. The round is not over yet."

"Listen!" the boy insisted. "If we don't get out of here, we're going to die. You don't know what's back there. It could come here any minute."

More contestants started gathering around me. The American seemed to recognize what was going on and tried to push through the crowd to reach me.

Suddenly, a sharp static noise pierced my ear drum. I pressed my finger against the earpiece and jerked my head away in pain.

"N-N-Nikki-cha-an …" a robotic voice sounded from the com.

"Moshi moshi?" I cupped my mouth to the side. Kuma Hunters tapped at their ears, some taking out their coms to examine them. The static noise continued. "Director?"

"What's happening?" voices mumbled.

"Y-yo-you n-ne-eed to ge-et…contestants…o-o-of-the-e-ere…shhhhh."

"What? Hello? Director? Are you there?" I yanked the earpiece out of my ear and the boy slapped it out of my hand. "Hey!"

His eyes landed on the megaphone behind me, and he whirled past me before I could stop him.

"We all need to go, now!" he screamed into the megaphone.

I gestured for a handful of Kuma Hunters to help me out. "All contestants must stay put!" I yelled over the growing commotion.

"Ahh!" A few contestants seized their head in pain, dropping to the floor, as though having a seizure.

"Make it stop!" The boy with the rod dropped the megaphone and fell to his knees.

"Something's wrong." The American pushed through the contestants.

The slip-and-counter of the contestants caused everyone to start running. A man with blood trickling from his ears grabbed a rifle from a quivering Kuma Hunter and aimed at a tree with a red-flashing device. I recognized it as a sonic weapon. "Don't!" I cried to the man.

He fired.

BOOM!

A blast wave vibrated through the forest. A fuse blew up from the digital clock and sparks rained over the field. Flames burst from the security office and contestants screamed. A tree split in half and collapsed in the center of the base. The fire spread from tree to tree, encircling everyone.

"Everybody run! Seek shelter!" I shouted. "The contestants!" I called for the remaining Kuma Hunters. Young contestants ran into me and I got lost in the crowd. I lunged forward and onto my knees. Someone stomped over my hand and sprinted over the fire behind. Another kicked me in the stomach, and as my head spun, hands wrapped around my arms and jerked me up.

"Are you okay?" the American asked, carrying the boy with the rod over his back. I touched my aching forehead. Blood trickled down. "Wh … at?" Another blast sounded off from the forest. A beech tree with orange and yellow lit leaves swayed over.

"Duck!" The American grabbed my waist and hurled me away. The tree crashed by my feet. "We need a way out," he said. The boy continued to twitch on the American's back.

"What's wrong with him?" I asked.

"Drop him," a voice ordered.

I squinted through the smoke to see a pony-tailed girl with claws. I recognized her as Maya. "He's one of the Kan," she said. "Drop him."

"What?!" The American yelled. "I know this boy and he's not with the Kan."

People on fire screamed around us. My head throbbed and my eyes blurred in and out of focus. The air smelt of smoke and burning flesh. Ash and debris filled my lungs. A cough surged out of my throat. "We're not going to make it alive if we keep bickering around."

"She's right," Maya said. "Give me the boy."

"Listen lady," the American shouted. "If this boy was with the Kan, I would know about it."

"Maya!" We heard a shriek from a boy with streaks of flame burning on his shoulder.

"Celio?" Her eyes widened. Several spots on the boy's back lit into flames. She patted them hard.

"Where's Eli?" His eyes searched the surroundings. "You left her?" He tackled Maya to the ground.

"Let's go!" the American said, ushering me with him. We saw the man with bear skin shout at the contestants. Ten others like him helped the injured, including Aya and her bodyguard.

"Goro!" The American waved at the man.

"Follow me!" Goro yelled. We dashed towards them, leaving Maya and the boy behind.

"We need to cross over the water," Goro said. "It's the only thing the fire won't go through."

"I know how to get there," I said, panting. We ran under a spreading canopy of red and orange. Wild boars and horned feral goats ran towards us from every direction. Golden eagles cawed in the distance. The wild flames licked over blackened bodies, and some of us tripped over them. The fire raged behind us and we crashed into a fence. Goro and his men helped everyone climb over to the other side. The American pushed me up the fence as I fell over. I helped him bring the boy with the rod down.

"Over here!" A man on the other side of a lake waved a torch in the air. "Whatever you do, stay away from the center," his voice echoed.

We ran into the cool water, swimming and dragging people with us. The boy's twitching had come to a stop as he slumped over the American's back. I swam along with them, still having trouble focusing. I felt the grasps of another around my waist, and two hands hauled me out of the water.

"This way!" An old man with hair dangling from his face and a scar under his eye waved his torch for everyone to see.

Goro and his friends helped more people up to the dry ground. The old man's torch pointed at the American's face. "Nick!" He said, running to him. "Did you see a b…"

The American slumped down on his knees, sliding the boy off his back. The old man rested a hand on the fishing rod and grasped the boy's face. "Shouta? My boy," he wept. "Y-you're alive."

I turned around to the fire enveloping everything in its way.

"Where are we?" the American asked me.

The screams died down, replaced by the dawning fear and whimpers of the contestants around me. "Welcome to the second round."

CHAPTER FIFTEEN

Celio

"HOW COULD YOU?" I YELLED. "I trusted you!" I tightened my grip around Maya's shoulders.

"She ran away looking for you," Maya explained. "Enura went to find h— Look out!" Maya aimed a kunai behind my back, and a man dropped to the ground. "The Kan are everywhere! You have to go! Go find your sister. I'll deal with them."

I ducked under the flying steel, merging with the running crowd. More men surrounded Maya as she fought them off.

"Eli!" I shouted, checking the burning bodies on the ground. The dead faces of strangers left me with the smallest glimmer of hope. I rushed through the running crowd diving over the fence and into the water. They carried me with them. Some shoved by me, others swam to the other side, but one remained calm at the bottom of a tree, a little girl with her still blue eyes reflecting the chaos.

"Eli!" I shrieked, paralyzed by the horror. My legs buckled, knees sinking into the sodden earth. "Dios mio…t-this can't be happening." My trembling hands splashed into her icy blood, taking hold of a kunai in her chest, and wrapping around her unmoving face. Grief surged with every breath. I cradled her in my arms, tears flowing from my helpless eyes and onto her chestnut hair. She didn't volunteer for this, she may have not been able to fend for herself, but she was strong, stronger than me. "This can't be happening…" I cried, rocking back and forth. "The Mori will pay. They will all pay for what they did to you, what they did to us!"

I saw a figure man rise from the black water lake heading in the opposite direction people ran in. His knee twitched, and a crack of the bone put it back to place. The torn, wet fabrics of his black clothes flapped around his staggering legs and arms. He heaved his head backward and his long black hair clapped against his back, blending in with the rest of him. He inched closed to me and my eyes fell on a bear tooth dangling from a chain around his neck.

"Stay back!" I shouted, closing my eyes. I silenced my jagged breathing as I clasped the kunai between my hands and pulled it away from Eli's chest. I pointed it at the man. "Don't come any closer!"

With slender arms, the man lifted Eli onto one shoulder, and pulled me onto another. "Let me go!" I kicked. "Where are you taking me? Put me down, o-or I'll kill you!"

CHAPTER SIXTEEN

Maya

"THE FIRE IS SPREADING FAST!" Enura skidded behind me, kicking a man in the stomach. A flying fist hurtled towards me. I grabbed it and twisted it as I hauled my legs around the man's neck, plummeting down to the ground on top of him.

"Is that all of them?" Enura asked.

"Eli isn't with you?"

"I couldn't find her anywhere." Enura shook his head. "She must have strayed far from the base."

"This is not good." I rested my palm against the bark of a tree. I had never felt this tired before. My chest heaved and my throat tightened. "This is like Italy all over again."

A shadow cut through the flames, slumping toward us.

"Enura!" it yelled. Two more figures dashed

through the flames behind it. "Get away from her." They came to a stop, a few feet away.

"Jun? Masaki?" I identified them along with a Kuma Hunter. Masaki spun his chains around him.

"What's going on?" Enura asked. "I thought you went after the Triplets."

"We did," Masaki spat. "Until that sonic blast got to them. We couldn't find them afterwards. She was one of them all along." The blades in his chains quivered and the color of the flames glimmered off his dilated pupils. Jun and the Kuma Hunter pointed their rifles at me.

"What do you mean?" Enura asked.

"Tell him what you told us," Jun said to the hunter.

"They found her hair on Oji-san's body," the Kuma Hunter said. "He's dead."

"W-what?" My voice lodged in my throat.

"We have to bring her in," the Kuma Hunter said.

"Are you crazy?! She didn't do that!" Enura yelled back. "We need to get her out of here. We need to all get out of here before we suffocate"

"Not with her I won't." Masaki took a step toward us.

"Masaki," Enura raised his hands in the air. "You need to calm down."

"Back off, Enura!" Masaki pointed the blades at him. "B-Back off! Do you know what this snake did? She pretended to be one of us! She lied to us!"

"Ok, Masaki." Enura backed away slowly. He tried to circle behind him, but Masaki whipped a kunai at him. It slashed his leg. Enura slanted to the side.

"Are you with her?" Masaki yelled at Enura.

"Calm down, Masaki." I held my arms up over my head. "We can talk about this. This is just the venom coursing in you."

"Oji-san is dead!" Masaki screamed at the top of his lungs. "Oji-san…is…d-dead!" Tears rolled down his cheeks, flying off his face.

"Shinjirarenai…" I uttered. "I don't believe it." I leaned back against the tree, my eyes burning red from the smoke.

"She killed him." Masaki pointed to at me. "She lied to us."

"No…" I muttered. "I didn't…it wasn't."

"Masaki." Enura walked towards him. "Do you even hear what you're saying? If she was with them, why would she help us take down the Kan?"

"To make us think she's on our side!" Masaki screamed.

"It's true," Jun added. "The Kan wouldn't mind killing off some of their own."

"They found a…hair at the lab," Masaki continued. "They say it's hers. It's a match. They found. Her. Hair. On. Oji-san's dead body! She did it! She framed it to look like he had a heart attack." Masaki lunged at me but his kunai clanked against Enura's.

"You will not touch her," Enura said.

"Get out of my way. She's a traitor! Mori-san was a fool to trust her. It's just like what Mother said, once a snake always a snake! Now back away, Enura."

"No."

"What?" Masaki's eyes wavered.

"You can't be possibly protecting Maya right now," Jun said. "If this is all true—"

"And if it's not? Do you want innocent blood on your hands? Huh?!"

"She's not innocent." Jun hesitated. "She killed all those innocent people in Italy. She started the fire there, and she did it here again."

"It's true," I spoke. "I was the one behind the fire."

Enura looked back at me. I grabbed onto his arm to back away from the tree. "It's okay, Enura. They have the right to be frightened."

"But you didn't do it. You didn't kill Oji-san," Enura insisted.

I nodded.

"Enura, Enura, Enura." Jun shook his head. "From the moment this pretty girl walked in, you haven't been able to take your eyes off her."

"You believe her word over mine?" Masaki choked. "After all we've been through together, how could you believe the words of a Kan?"

"Whether she's with the Kan or not, all I know is that she didn't do it."

"Get out of our way, Enura. Otherwise you're going down with her." Jun pointed his rifle at Enura.

"Maya," Enura whispered while pushing me back. "Go."

"No." I tightened my fingers around the hilt of my blade. "I don't want you to die because of me."

Enura snickered. "You really think these two idiots can kill me? You underestimate me too much." He turned around to block Masaki's attacks while Jun shot after me. "Run!" Enura shouted. Masaki swung at Enura. He dodged, spun around and elbowed him. He kicked the rifle out of Jun's hands and the Kuma Hunter hurried after me.

I leaped over the flames and ducked under falling branches. Bullets whizzed over my head. I heard the propellers of a helicopter above, and saw it fly over with a water tank. Sweat seeped through my clothes and my skin burned like the fire had already reached me. The hammering in my chest made it hard to breathe as tendrils of grey smoke swirled into my lungs. Cool interlocked metal brought a sweet rush to my fingers. I clambered over the fence and hid behind a tree. The Kuma Hunter rattled the fence and scanned the field. I watched him run down a slope. Relieved, I turned around and a blow struck the back of my head. I staggered forward, my mind swirling, and my breaths shallow. Fading screams for help echoed in my ears and feeling in my body drained away until all was black.

EPILOGUE

A BLACK WOODPECKER FLIES OVER the fire. Its pupils zoom in and out of focus, reflecting the retreating contestants. It blinks.

"Shut it off!" Mrs. Kimura yells at the Director, standing up from her chair.

A young man pauses the surveillance footage on the screen. "The coms are still down," he says. "Whatever it was, it might take some time to get the audio back on."

"What about my daughter?" Hideki-san, in another chair, yells. "Was she on any of the footage?"

"She wasn't among the dead, thank god," the Director says. "She escaped with the others."

"Here," Mrs. Kimura tucks a badge in Mr. Hideki's chest pocket. "She's going to need this."

Mr. Hideki raises the badge to his face and gapes at its number. "My daughter's badge…h-how?"

"Let's just say I made a new friend." Mrs. Kimura

grins, and brings her lips to his ear. "She was dead, or at least I thought she was the last time. No matter, I can bring her back." And, turning to the young man, "hook me up," she orders. The young man attaches a cable to her tablet. She rewinds the footage and freezes it on a ponytailed girl with claws. "Interesting."

The Director snaps his fingers at the young man to pour everyone some tea. The clock on the wall ticks over to 8AM. Mrs. Mori walks in, no longer wearing a blindfold. Scarred tissue stretches around her eyes, and two blue circles shine like two vivid points, but they don't see. She has no pupils.

"My dear!" Mrs. Kimura lowers the tablet, and fixes her eyes on Mrs. Mori. "Fire just seems to follow you wherever you go. What a sight, ah-forgive me for using that word." She covers a grin that stretches across her face. "Such beauty gone like that. I could do something about that skin."

Mrs. Mori taps her cane for silence. "Where are we on the contestants?" she asks.

"Making their way to the tower as we speak," the Director responds.

"My dear, you shouldn't worry about the contestants when you have your family to take care of."

Mrs. Kimura sips her tea, taking a seat and folding her legs. "I'm sure your father in-law's heart attack has left you restless."

"His killer has been apprehended," Mrs. Mori stares at her blankly.

"Really?" Mrs. Kimura lowers her cup. "Who was it?"

"It's being taken care of."

***

In a dark room, barely six feet by four, chains hang from a thick grey-stoned wall. Instead of a door, metal bars line the opening to the hollow cube of the concrete prison. There's no sound, light, or furniture of any kind. A thick stench of festering sewage drafts in every few moments.

A ponytailed girl twitches, a heavy metal chain wound all around her body. Manacles fix two rings on her neck: one attached to the chain, the other hanging from two irons reaching to her waist. A padlock secures her hands. Her eyes suddenly open and she takes in her surroundings. She can neither raise her hands to her mouth nor lower her head to her hands. Across from her, in another hollow cube concrete, another chain encircles the neck of a silver-streaked head. This man stares at her as she struggles to break free. She catches his gaze and freezes.

"Minoru?"

He averts his eyes.

"It-it's me, Maya. W-where are we?"

"The basement."

"W-why are you in chains? Does your mother know? Did she put you in there?"

"I walked into it of my own free will," he says. "To make up for my sins. What about you?"

About the Author

I'm an aspiring author and screenwriter currently living in different parts of the world. Since 2015, I've been travelling and experiencing collective living with friends, family and even strangers with one thing in common—meditation. I'm an active member and a volunteer for Sahaja Yoga Meditation, founded by H.H. Shri Mataji Nirmala Devi. I love traveling to SY seminars, festivals, concerts, even volunteering at schools for Inner Peace Day. For more information, visit www.katherinenader.com